BITTER
Tastes

*To Sara —
Enjoy the ride!
VBRosendahl*

V. B. Rosendahl

Bitter Tastes is a work of fiction. Any resemblance to actual
persons and/or events is strictly coincidental. References to
actual places and/or historic events are meant to enhance the
story and provide a realistic setting for the novel.

Requests for permission to make copies of any part of the
work should be mailed to:
Stargazer Press
33 Patton Rd.
Barrie, ON
L4M 1H6
Canada

Cover design is by Paul Hughes. Editing is by Tina Musial.
Text layout is by Fine Line Design.

Library and Archives Canada Cataloguing in Publication

Rosendahl, Victoria, 1956-
    Bitter tastes / Victoria Rosendahl.

ISBN 0-9734940-9-3
    I. Title.
PS3618.O824B58 2006   j813'.6   C2006-900458-7

Printed in Canada

This book is dedicated to kids, young and old, all over the world. If you love to read, I hope it inspires you to read more and even write your own mysteries. If you haven't yet fallen in love with reading, perhaps you will someday and I hope this book helped lead you to it.

Readers of this tale have my undying gratitude for their support. You guys are the most important part of this process.

No book is ever written by one person. If it takes a village to raise a child, it takes an army to write a book. A big thank-you goes to Kim Leggett, the first one to read the raw manuscript and see its potential. Next is my sister-in-law, Janet Dolan, who exclaimed, "You write so clean!" She inspired me to turn this novel into a mystery for kids.

I couldn't have found the right voice without readers like Mike Adams who told me when my 11-year-old terminology was off base or Caroline Selby who helped me see the error of some of my pre-teen character's ways.

A huge thanks to Robyn Whyte and Stargazer Press whose hard work and dedication are getting this book into the hands of lots of people.

Finally, I can never write a novel without the support of my best friend, Matt. He's the greatest husband (and fan) a girl could ask for. He always believes in me … even when I don't quite believe in myself.

For more information about VB Rosendahl, please visit her website at www.vbrosendahl.com.

CHAPTER ONE

I CAN TELL YOU EXACTLY WHEN I became afraid. I'm not talking about the story-by-the-campfire-willies. I mean hair-standing-up-on-the-neck scared. My stomach churned when Martha Cunningham dragged me into this nasty doublewide trailer. And then I saw it.

The murder weapon.

Now, others may not have known it for what it was but I did. It sat on an end table like a prize won at a Virginia turkey-shoot. In fact, someone might call it an abstract piece of art but it really belonged in the kitchen.

The eyes of four of my sixth grade classmates watched me intently, begging me to continue my story.

Let me introduce myself first. I'm Kathy Harmon and you already know my sidekick Martha Cunningham. I could say that it was Martha who got us into this but that wouldn't be quite true. She did, however, get us into the trailer.

The trailer was a dump on the outside and that should have been my first clue as to what life was like on the inside. An awning made it only halfway to the picnic table it was supposed to shade. A large rip in the canvas saw to that. Several discolored plastic chairs were gathered around a yellowing table. And the trailer's white exterior was brown with rust.

"This is stupid, Martha. You saw the look on his face yesterday." I whispered this to her as we snuck up to the trailer. It was surrounded by tangled brush and long forgotten beer cans.

"Look, Kathy, I have a feeling about this. Just follow my lead." Martha motioned me to follow her around back. Two broken concrete steps led to a torn screen door. The porch light remained on even in the middle of the day.

I'll end up following your lead into a lifetime of being grounded, I thought. "Sure, okay," I said, copying her foot-steps for fear of stepping in some trap.

"What if he's here?" I asked, grabbing Martha's arm.

"He's not."

"But what if he comes home and finds us?"

"Then we're toast." The back door opened when she turned the knob. "Moron," she said.

We went inside. Newspapers and take-out bags were scattered all over the living room floor. A week's worth of dishes were stacked in the sink. And, fortunately, there was no dead body. I've watched enough TV and read enough mysteries to know that dead bodies stink. This trailer smelled a lot like my Gran's house: dusty mothballs.

I heard Martha call for me but I refused to move an inch from inside the front door. Each time she called to me she got louder.

I caved and slowly walked in the direction of Martha's voice. This could be really stupid. How did I get into such a mess? I soon found Martha on the threshold of a shrine to Janine McKellum. Dead Janine McKellum. Pictures and articles plastered the bedroom walls.

"Holy smokes, Marth. This guy's nuts. Let's get out of here."

"In a sec," she answered, heading back down the hall to the living room. "Jeeze," she said, as she kicked a can to the side, "doesn't this dude ever clean?"

I resumed my watch at the front door. "Maybe he could hire your Mom to come in and straighten up."

"Maybe I could," came the booming voice of the trailer's

owner as he pushed me out of the way. I landed on all fours, heart pounding. Martha chose this moment to clam up. "Now I got both of you for breaking and entering."

I remained frozen to my spot and tried to breathe again. I tried to focus on something, anything, to regain some calm. It didn't work. Being on my stomach put me face-to-face with Martha's feet. Seeing her little toes peeking out of holes in her sneakers reminded me of the day we had first met.

CHAPTER TWO

I MET MARTHA CUNNINGHAM on the day I had dreaded all summer long: the first day of school. And it wasn't just any first day of school. It was the first day in a new school. My first day in a new school in a new state. And I didn't know anybody. I hated being new.

I dressed that morning, slowly, hoping that Mom and Dad would tell me I didn't have to go. Wrong. The only thing Mom said as I walked into the kitchen was, "Learn well! We're in paradise!"

Sure, she thought we were in paradise. When they told me two months ago that we were moving I thought they meant to the house my Dad had wanted for years. In a different neighborhood, not in a different state. But then we moved all the way to Warner, North Carolina, a beach community on the Outer Banks, and I knew that I had really done something bad to deserve this.

It was okay for vacations, when there were things to do like go shelling and hang out in the little shops. But to actually move here and live year-round when most everything closes up after Labor Day? I just knew that my folks had snapped their caps.

My mother, not the happiest person in the world, turned nice at the same time my father sold the liquor store for one point two million dollars. That put a real smile on her face. And we left New Jersey. She hated New Jersey. She loved North Carolina.

When I got to school that first day I stood just outside the playground. Watching kids I had never seen before play in the sand (yes, sand) made me feel shy. I glanced around to see if anyone was watching and then racked my bike and locked it up.

I really hated being new.

You know what that's like: the awful combination of wanting to be included while at the same time being invisible. I made doubly sure that my deformed left hand was tucked safely into the pocket of my shorts. A new kid sticks out. A new kid in a small-town school sticks out more. And a new kid with no fingers on her left hand was the worst.

"Hey, Cunningham!" yelled a girl's loud voice from behind me. I hoped no one had seen me jump. Two girls brushed past me as though I weren't there and a third turned at the mention of her name.

Martha Cunningham smiled broadly and didn't seem self-conscious about her crooked two front teeth. The three girls giggled together and while I imagined their sharing of summer stories, I also wondered where someone goes on vacation when living in paradise.

I turned and walked in the front doors of Warner School. "Hi, Kathy! Welcome!" I hoped that another Kathy stood right behind me but I realized it wasn't true when my sixth grade teacher, Miss Fiddler, joined me. Luckily, another student chimed in before I could answer. It gave me just enough time to move away so no one would see me talking to a teacher. Being seen talking to a teacher was a fate worse than zits back home in New Jersey.

"Hey, Miss Fiddler," said a tall boy. "My Mom wants to know if you're gonna tutor again this year."

"Hi, Michael. Yes. Tell her I will. You interested?"

"Yes. Definitely. Math. I'm not so good at math."

"Okay. Let's talk more at lunch. Whose class are you in this year?"

"Mrs. Langham's. You think she'd mind if I got tutored by my teacher from last year?" The boy towered over Miss Fiddler. He wore the latest in baggy clothes.

"Whoa, Michael, you sure jumped up this summer. Mike, I'd like you to meet a new sixth grade student, Kathy Harmon. From New Jersey." By the time Miss Fiddler made the introduction I had disappeared into a sea of faces. I couldn't yet deal with kids in my own class let alone a seventh-grader.

I found the perfect place near the girl's bathroom to watch and see which room Miss Fiddler went into so I could find it without looking totally lost. As I followed her I just knew that I would end up sitting in the front row.

Room 6 was like nothing I had ever seen before. Desks took up most of the space but soft chairs formed a reading area in back. A jigsaw puzzle sat on a nearby table. I stood at the door as other students walked in around me. I could hear the sounds of an aquarium and, when I looked up, saw brightly colored kites hanging from the ceiling.

"Hi," came a voice from directly behind me. I turned to find Martha Cunningham smiling at me.

"Uh, hi," I said. Brilliant. I sounded so smart. My first word was "uh".

"I'm Martha," she said, extending her hand toward me. I didn't respond in kind. "You in Fiddler's class?"

"Yeah." More brilliance.

"Cool. See ya." Martha breezed past me and into the room.

"Okay guys. Let's go," said Miss Fiddler as she rounded up the remaining students. They had all found their desks and that left me with, you guessed it, the first row. I tried to look cool as I sat up front but knew that my face had already reddened at the thought of being planted right in front of the teacher.

CHAPTER THREE

THE MORNING FLEW BY, packed with first day activities. After lunch, the sun melted into the clouds threatening another late summer thunderstorm. I don't know if I'll ever get used to having to go back to school in August. I liked what we did at my old school: after Labor Day.

Miss Fiddler took that opportunity to discuss weather and hurricanes. "Okay. When we went out to lunch and recess did you notice the sky?" No one volunteered to answer. "When you came to school this morning what was the day like? Kathy?"

Please, please, PLEASE let there be another Kathy in the room. No such luck. "Sunny?" I answered softly.

"Yes. Good." Miss Fiddler smiled at me encouragingly. "Now what is it like?"

"Cloudy?"

"Is it? Is it really cloudy?"

I thought about this question with everything I had, as though this were the question that would land me in the record books. I'm sure that I wasn't fooling anyone, least of all Miss Fiddler.

"It's certainly becoming cloudy, more so than this morning. What's causing that do you think?" The class remained still, silent. "All right, folks, dig out your science books."

I noticed that Martha Cunningham sat only two seats away from me. She spoke as we took out our books. I turned to look in her direction then and saw a silver bracelet slide down her arm as she raised her hand higher. That's when I first noticed the holes in her sneakers that made her baby toes stick out and the wear in her cut-offs.

"Miss Fiddler?" asked Martha. "I have a question."

"Is it about weather?"

"No."

Miss Fiddler sighed. "Okay. But let's make it a short one." The students around me snickered. Miss Fiddler leaned against the chalkboard and crossed her arms in front of her.

"Why are funerals so important? My Mom said that she has to go to a funeral tomorrow. Why?"

Miss Fiddler looked at Martha. Before she could answer Martha spoke again.

"I mean, really, why don't parents tell us what's going on? Do they think we're dumb or something? I'm eleven and a quarter. I understand stuff." My mother would call Martha precocious.

"Have you told your Mom that?"

"Yeah, well, sort of. Whenever I ask about death and stuff she tells me I'm too young to understand." Two or three other students agreed.

"Death is part of life. Funerals are rituals for the living not for the dead. The dead couldn't care less." It felt good to laugh along with the class. "Some like to call it closure," Miss Fiddler continued. "It's a rationalization."

"What's that?" asked Martha.

"It's when you try to tell yourself something is okay so you'll feel better. Sometimes rationalizations are fine; other times they help make you feel better when you're hurting. Like, let's say that you and your best friend just had a huge fight. You tell yourself it's for the best, there'll be other best friends, that sort of thing. That's a rationalization. But you're really hurting inside and think that your old best friend was the only one who would ever understand you."

Boy could I identify with that! Like my Mom trying to talk me into being happy about moving away from New Jersey and my friends, Curtis and Stephanie. Or when my Mom talked my Dad into selling the store, telling him it would be for the best when she made him take the first offer. They don't know that I know that about them, but I do. I agreed with Martha; we're not dumb. We understand a whole lot more than parents give us credit for.

"Thanks Miss Fiddler," said Martha. "So what funeral is it?"

"Whose funeral, not what funeral. Janine McKellum. She owned Janine's Restaurant." Miss Fiddler's voice broke.

I had already read about it in the evening paper and felt sad. She had been my only friend in paradise. Miss Janine taught the summer "Kooking with Kids" class that my Mom made me take. I thought she was cool. She was teaching me to recognize the different herbs and spices in her small back-yard garden and what dishes went with each. I felt fresh tears start to sting my eyes. I liked her. And I think she liked me. She had helped me feel like a girl with two good hands.

"You okay Miss Fiddler?" asked Norm Parkey, who startled me back to the present.

"Yes. Yeah, sure. Miss McKellum was an old friend. We went to high school together back in the dark ages. I miss her."

"Did she really have her skull bashed in?" asked Norm.

I gasped and clamped a hand over my mouth. I felt others staring at me so I slid down in my seat, trying to be invisible. I looked up from staring at my lap and saw Miss Fiddler watching me.

"I don't know. What did you hear about it Norm?"

I turned to look at Norm who sat one row back from me. His brown eyes were full of excitement at being able to tell this latest piece of dirt like he had just caught a foul ball at a Mets game. "Well," he said, sitting up straighter, "I heard that Miss Janine stole some stuff and she got conked on the head for it."

I looked hard to see Miss Fiddler's reaction. Her eyebrows furrowed and she looked tired suddenly. "Let's talk about this," she said as she sat on the corner of her desk. She swung one tanned foot back and forth and then, for the first time that day, I noticed Miss Fiddler's clothes. She wore a pair of cargo shorts with a cotton shirt and sandals.

"Can anyone tell me what a rumor is?" Miss Fiddler asked.

The boy sitting next to me raised his hand.

"Yes, Jeb," she said, pointing at him.

"A rumor is when you say something about somebody but you don't know that it's true."

"Good. Do you have to repeat it?"

"Well, yeah. If you don't tell it to someone it would be just your own information. My Dad says that a rumor is like poop. You don't want to step in it and you don't want to spread it around."

I liked him already. I glanced at him out of the corner of my eye. He was kind of cute.

Miss Fiddler smiled. "You tell your Dad I like that one, Jeb. What Norm just said about Miss Janine isn't true. I've known her for a long time and I have never known her to be anything but honest."

Wait a minute, I thought. Isn't what Miss Fiddler just said a rumor? Just as I was starting to raise my hand, Martha broke in.

"But isn't what you just said a rumor?" asked Martha. I looked over at her and raised my eyebrows.

"No, I don't think so. Why?"

"Do you know for sure that she didn't steal anything?"

"No. I don't. I'm assuming she didn't because of my friendship with her. But, Martha, you're right. You used logic. Good job." Martha smiled broadly. I smiled, too, feeling the victory as well.

"I heard that Miss Janine and Mr. Otto were lovers!" exclaimed Norm.

I shivered at that thought. Mr. Otto was a million years old and managed Janine's Restaurant.

"This isn't an appropriate subject for class, Norm. Where do you get this stuff?"

"Reruns of Melrose Place!"

"Your Mom lets you watch that?"

"She works nights. She don't know——-"

Miss Fiddler stopped him right there. "Doesn't. Doesn't know."

"She doesn't know."

"Okay. Enough."

Norm Parkey said, "This is way cool, Miss Fiddler."

"Because you mentioned sex, Norm?"

"Well, yeah, partly."

"Yeah, right, Parkey," said Martha. As she said this Martha looked right at me and smiled. I smiled back thinking that maybe this wouldn't be so bad after all.

CHAPTER FOUR

J UST WHEN I THOUGHT THINGS might be okay in paradise, life threw me one of those lemons my mother had told me about. Her favorite saying these days had something to do with getting lemons and making lemonade. I'm not really sure what she meant but I think it had something to do with making the best out of a bad situation.

Afternoon recess came after our science lesson. I looked up at the semi-cloudy sky (I still thought it was cloudy despite what Miss Fiddler said) and wondered when the rain might come. Kids in my class were choosing up sides for dodge ball.

"I'll take Parkey," said Jeb, after being named captain of the blue team.

"Cunningham," said a girl with bright green eyes, heading up the yellow team.

It was at that moment that Martha Cunningham blew my cover. Before I could protest, she came to my side, yanked my left hand out of its hiding place in my shorts pocket and threw that hand in the air exclaiming, "Pick Kathy! She's great!" The sight of my left hand, fingerless from the first knuckle up with a deformed thumb, drew a gasp from the collected crowd. And this caused Martha to look at what they had seen.

I could tell that she was instantly embarrassed not only from the slackness of her jaw but by the redness in her face. I put my hand back in my pocket as fast as humanly possible, hoping that no one had taken a really good look. It was bad enough to be new; being new and deformed was more than most kids could take.

The game selection process went on until everyone was chosen. Except me.

"Hey. What's your name?" Jeb said to me.

"Um, Kathy?" When I felt uncertain and small my answers sometimes came out like questions.

"Well, um Kathy, we have enough for each side. Sit this one out, okay?"

I saw him look down at my left shorts pocket and then at me. The look in his eyes told me that he didn't want me on his team. It seemed as though all of the kids were staring at me, waiting for my response.

"Sure thing," I said, as strongly as I could muster. I knew deep down in my heart that my agreement had come out wimpier than I wanted it to.

I took a seat on a nearby bench and watched as my classmates enjoyed themselves.

"I'll never fit in here," I whispered.

CHAPTER FIVE

I SAT ALONE IN MY ROOM AFTER SUPPER dreading the second day of school. I thought about Miss Janine. The evening paper had run an article about the funeral and I was surprised to see her age listed as 43. She seemed a lot younger that that.

The first time I met her she was all sweaty from a long night of cooking. My parents had taken me to eat at her restaurant. I thought it would be food that only adults liked, but Janine made sure kids had their own menu that included burgers and chicken tenders and fries.

My Mom had seen the ads for "Kooking with Kids" classes and signed me up not long after moving to paradise. I had barely unpacked before she roped me into "activities". I'll admit it, but only to you, that I was wrong about the cooking classes. I thought they were going to be this horribly boring two-hour ordeal with some old lady. But Miss Janine was cool. I learned new things that I probably never would have had I not done this. But please don't tell my Mom that I said that, okay?

I liked to hang out after class and help with the food prep for the restaurant. Miss Janine would let me do this every once in a while. Thinking back on it now, the last day I saw her was the day she died.

I remember standing at one of the deep sinks doing some dishes when a loud man banged through the screen door. Because I'm short, I needed to stand on a stool in order to reach into the sink and I was lifting a heavy platter when he came roaring in.

"Janine!" he screamed as he threw open the screen door. "Janine! Get out here this second!" His voice was the kind of low rumble you hear on a boom box. He disappeared around the corner into the dining room before I could see what he looked like.

"Give it to me, Janine," he continued. I wiped my soapy hands on the short green apron tied around my waist and jumped down from the stool to get a better look. I inched up to the same corner he had just gone around and listened, quietly poking my nose into their business.

"No!" shouted Janine. "That was my grandmother's favorite platter, Connor. You know how much it means to me."

"And you know how much that recipe means to me." I heard the platter shatter to bits. That's when I looked around the corner. Connor looked like an angry cartoon character and I clamped a hand over my mouth to keep from laughing out loud at him.

My laughter quickly flipped to surprise as I watched Janine react to the shattering of old porcelain and memories. She lunged for Connor, caught him off guard and knocked him down. Coins and a pair of glasses spilled from his pocket.

I didn't know what to do. Should I interrupt, little-girl like, and hope to stop them from hurting each other? There was no one else in the restaurant but the three of us and I was too small to help. But he was being mean to my friend. He scrambled to his feet and started to walk away.

"Connor!" shouted Janine. "Don't you dare run away from me after what you did!"

No one had noticed me yet.

Connor turned and hissed. "You have embarrassed me, Janine. I have warned you never to do that. Never!" This guy was taller than Miss Janine by at least a head and he stood so close to her that she had to crane her neck just to look at him.

"Don't you recall what happened the last time you disobeyed me?" he asked. "Have you forgotten so quickly?"

A shiver ran up my spine.

"I'm sick of you," Janine whispered.

"You're a thief, Janine. A common criminal."

"And you can't read."

"I created the torta rustica recipe you're using and I'll contact the European competition officials about that. I'll ruin you."

"You're dyslexic and have been faking it for years. Merely pretending to read with your gaudy glasses. You wouldn't know if the recipe I'm using is yours or not."

By this time I'd stretched my neck around the corner to watch the action. I could see by the reaction on Connor's face that Janine's last remark had hit home hard. The smirk she wore must have been the trigger that made him explode because he pushed her back against a sideboard hutch. When he grabbed her by the throat I nearly lost it. I gasped and ducked back around the corner hoping they hadn't heard me.

"So you do remember what happened last time, hmm? Don't you dare threaten me, little girl. I'll crush you. And don't go looking for Scottie Fiddler or Ray Corcoran to rescue you like they did when you were kids."

This guy's bananas. And they obviously had been at this before. And now I knew a little more. I had had friends who got smacked around and this must be the same thing only in adult-size. I wondered if Miss Janine and this Connor character had ever been more than friends. Must have been. Otherwise why would she have let this happen before?

Connor clearly over-powered her by height, weight and brute strength. "You ready to surrender?" I heard him ask Miss Janine. She didn't respond and he pushed harder. "Remove the recipe from your menu immediately or we'll have another discussion."

Oh, boy. I knew a good cue when I heard one. I chose that moment to walk around the corner and into the line of fire. "Miss Janine?" I asked sweetly. "I need some help." I cut my sentence off just right and stood there, gaping at the tableau formed by Connor and Janine against the hutch as though I were shocked.

Connor stared at me and back at Janine. "I'll be back to check on things," he warned before storming out of the dining room.

"You okay?" I asked.

"I'm fine, Kath." Janine rubbed her throat and I could see distinct finger marks. She began to pick up the pieces of the broken platter and I went to help. "Did you see much of that?"

"No," I lied.

"Good. Thanks."

"What happened? Did you drop a platter?"

"Yup. Wasn't careful." She didn't know how true that was.

"That platter was your Grandma's, wasn't it?" I watched Miss Janine stare at the last piece of porcelain. Tears formed in her eyes.

"It was. It was the last piece of her I had left."

"Who was that gorilla?"

Janine smiled at that remark.

"An old friend. We went to cooking school together after college. He runs the Old Salt Restaurant on Route 55."

As we took the pieces of the platter into the kitchen to dump them in the trash, I saw something in the corner. It was a pair of glasses with the ugliest frames I had ever seen. The colors reminded me of an old bruise: yellow, green, blue, red and purple. I picked them up and said, "Are these yours?"

"Huh?" She stared at the glasses I held in my hand. "Oh. No. Let's put them over here." Miss Janine took them from me and laid them in a well in between the stainless steel preparation counters.

"He didn't seem like much of a friend," I said to her.

Miss Janine turned and looked at me with sad eyes like a Bassett hound. "Sometimes friends aren't friends. You know?" A few quiet moments passed before she spoke again. "Want to help me in the garden?"

"Sure." Miss Janine looked shaken and small and I hoped that I could at least be good company.

∽

Earlier that summer, Miss Janine told me about her physical limitations. She became an even better friend than I could have hoped for.

"Do you want to talk about your hand?" she asked me one afternoon after class.

I hesitated a beat too long and that caused her to go on.

"You know, when I was in culinary school, I cut my hand so badly that I severed some nerves. There are parts of my right hand that I can't feel or use anymore and I really have to compensate for it in the kitchen."

I turned to look at her and then saw her outstretched palm. The scar ran right along her lifeline. She let me have a good, long look at it and then she asked to see mine. Reluctantly, I showed her the mangled mess that I knew was my left hand.

Miss Janine didn't say a word. I watched her closely as she examined my thumb and then my missing fingers. "Must be tough on you in this class. Need to do everything with your right hand."

I acknowledged her kindness with a nod.

"A friend of mine helped me do some exercises with the parts of my hand that still worked. Maybe we could devise the same strategy for you." I smiled at her gratefully and wondered if her "friend" Connor had anything to do with hurting her and then trying to help her.

CHAPTER SIX

FTER SUPPER ON THE FIRST DAY of school, I
decided to solve the mystery of who killed Miss
Janine. I took the evening newspaper along with a
blank notebook upstairs to my room. I clipped the articles
about the murder and taped them in a book now marked
"Who Killed Miss Janine?" and jotted some notes to myself
about what concerned me most, sort of like a diary. I began
to compile a list of suspects or I should say "suspect" because
the only one I had so far was Connor, the man I saw yelling
at Miss Janine.

Sitting in Room 6 after lunch the next day, I thought
about the photo of Otto von Blumm, the restaurant
manager, and Miss Janine on the day the restaurant had
opened in 1995. Both were smiling, standing in front of the
screened porch. Red geraniums in hanging pots made it look
cheerful. Was there something else in Miss Janine's eyes?
Was her smile not as real as it should be? I didn't know what
to think.

Well, it was a start. Last night's wind had blown the
clouds and rain away leaving a sparkling blue sky and fresh
on-shore breeze for my second day of school. I did not want
to go outside and try to play after what had happened
yesterday.

A jigsaw puzzle caught my eye. The lid showed a marina filled with boats. I stared at it while trying to put together the pieces of Miss Janine's puzzle in my head.

"I see you found it," Miss Fiddler said from the doorway.

I jumped in response to her voice and answered, "Oh. Yeah."

"Didn't feel like going outside to get some air?"

"I'm not very good at games," I lied. The truth was that I was pretty good at games despite my restrictions but just had too much on my mind.

"How's it going being new in town? Made some friends?"

I shook my head while turning a puzzle piece over in my hand.

"When I do one of these," Miss Fiddler said, "I look for the edge pieces first. Let's see what we can find."

Miss Fiddler and I looked over the table and she made the first move by placing two edge pieces in the center. "After I find all the edges I try to find the corners. Corners are pretty easy."

I rolled my eyes and tried to think of something to say. "I miss Miss Janine."

"Janine and I were close friends for a long time. I miss her, too."

"Why did this happen to her? She was so nice. She treated me like I had brains. I just don't understand why this kind of stuff happens to people. I thought this was paradise."

"Paradise, huh? Where did you get that idea?"

"My Mom. That's what she calls Warner. I guess it is compared to New Jersey." I kept talking in order to fish for more information. Don't get me wrong. Miss Janine's death upset me but I also wanted more to go on to solve the mystery.

"I don't know," Miss Fiddler said.

"Don't know what?"

"Why this happened to her. Warner is a pretty quiet little village. There isn't much crime and certainly no murders."

Before I knew it, Miss Fiddler and I had sorted out all of the edge pieces.

"What did you like most about Janine?" Miss Fiddler asked.

"She didn't make fun of me."

"Why on Earth would she make fun of you? You're nice and pretty and smart."

"She understood me. There are some things I can't do."

"Oh, everyone is like that. I have no depth perception."

"What's that?"

"Well, let's break the phrase down," she said, starting to be the teacher again. "What's depth?"

I knew this was the first real test with this teacher and wanted to impress her. "How tall or wide something is?" I answered hopefully.

"Close. What kind of wide?"

I narrowed my eyes at her not really catching on to her point.

Miss Fiddler spread her hands apart. "This kind of wide?"

The little light bulb went on over my head. Now I knew what she meant. "No," I said, "this kind of wide." I placed my right hand against my stomach and then ended with it against the edge of the puzzle table. "Deep. Not fat. Oh, right! Depth."

"Good. Now let's look at the other word. What is perception?"

"How you see something?"

"Right. So if I have no depth perception what would that mean?"

"You can't tell how deep something is?"

"Partly. What else is measured with depth?"

I looked up to the hanging kites for inspiration and prayed that this game would end soon.

"How about how far away something is?" Miss Fiddler prodded.

I smiled, now understanding the difference. "So, like, how do you drive? Do you have a lot of accidents?"

"You'd think so," she said with a chuckle. "No. I don't drive much here on the island. I prefer to walk or ride my bike. But when I do drive I just leave lots of room between me and the other cars."

"I can measure depth easy."

"Easily."

"Easily." I scoured the classroom for a good example. "From here to the blackboard is about thirty feet."

Miss Fiddler shook her head and said, "I have no clue. Couldn't even guess."

"You remind me of Miss Janine." I'm not sure what made me say that then except that it was true. Miss Fiddler's kindness reminded me of her.

"I do? Thanks."

We sat in silence for a while putting the edge pieces together to form the puzzle's frame. Miss Fiddler spoke first. "What is it that makes you different?"

"Well, my left hand—," I began but then stopped short when I saw Norm Parkey poke his head inside the classroom door.

"Hey! Cool! We're working on the puzzle, huh Miss Fiddler?" Norm asked. "Can I play too?"

"I've gotta go, Miss Fiddler," I said standing quickly. The last thing I needed was a string of questions from Nosy Norm.

CHAPTER SEVEN

I TROTTED DOWN THE HALLWAY and away from Room 6. I didn't know where I was going, just sure of where I didn't belong. As I rounded a turn in the hallway I smashed into this huge guy. At first I thought I had just made the biggest mistake of my life—first running in a school hallway and then crashing into a teacher. But he wasn't a teacher, I could tell that right off.

This huge man stood in front of the boys' bathroom with a wet mop in his hand. Next to me he seemed massive, certainly well over six feet tall.

"Hey, better watch out there, kiddo," he said. I stared at the name "John Tucker" sewn above the left pocket of his uniform. His booming voice hurt my ears a little and his attempt to soothe me came out too sticky sweet. Something inside told me not to trust him.

"Hey, Kath! There you are. I've been looking all over for you," said Martha Cunningham. "Oh, hi, Mr. Tucker," she added. Martha took me by the elbow, led me out of school and onto the sandy playground. I felt grateful for the rescue and would not forget her kindness.

Inhaling deeply, I looked at Martha. "Thank you. Thank you so much. I just, I don't know. He was the scariest thing I've ever seen!" More brilliance from Miss Harmon. First I greeted her yesterday with "uh" and now I sound like I'm about five years old around a campfire.

"Hey, Mr. Tucker ain't no day at the beach, you know? What do you think of Fiddler?" she asked, changing the subject. Right then another teacher walked by and gave Martha a scowl. "Miss Fiddler," Martha responded. The teacher smiled.

"I don't know what came over me. I feel like such a jerk." I pushed damp hair away from my face with both hands.

"After yesterday, I understand better why you do that."

"Um, do what?" I asked, trying to deflect the obvious questions.

"Keep your hand in your pocket so much."

I said nothing.

"It's okay. I won't tease you or anything. My Uncle Archie-bald had a false leg. Lost it in a land mine in Nam."

"Nam?"

"You know. Viet Nam? The war we never should've been in?" I failed to react so she continued. "The best time in the world! The sixties? I've got a lot to teach you," she said, shaking her head.

We sat, side by side, on the swings. I took off my sandals and dug my bare feet into the cool, comforting sand down under the warm first layer.

∼

That afternoon after school I took the plunge and invited Martha to my house. I worried a little about this because I knew my house was bigger than most houses in Warner. A lot of the houses were old and run-down but tourists thought they were cute.

We carried glasses filled with ice and two cans of soda

upstairs to my room. "This room is so cool," Martha said as we entered. I watched her stroll around its perimeter, looking first at the books on the shelves and then kneeling on the large window seat that had a view of the bay. She sat back and said, "You could have a dance in here!" My mother had said the exact same thing when we finished decorating it.

"Have you been talking to my mother?" I asked.

"Huh?"

"Nothing, nothing."

Martha continued her tour by opening up every possible door and drawer. She found the TV and VCR in a large chest in the corner. Then she went to my desk.

"Whoa! What's this? I've never seen anything like it." Martha stared down at the video monitor to my computer mounted underneath a piece of glass in the desktop.

"That's my computer for school."

"Isn't the monitor supposed to be on top of the desk?"

"My Dad had this desk built for me. He has one too. He thinks that looking down at the monitor is better for my eyes," I explained, desperate to change the subject. My parents' wealth was something I hadn't gotten used to yet.

"So what's with the bracelet?" I asked, pointing to her wrist.

Still examining the under-desk monitor, she responded, "It's an MIA bracelet."

"MIA?"

"Yeah. Missing in Action? MIA bracelets were the rage in the '60s during the war."

"Nam?"

"Right! People sent in money to help find soldiers who were missing and in return you got a bracelet with the name and date they were listed as missing. I got this one from my uncle."

I looked closely at the piece of silver Martha handed to me and read the inscription: "Commander Theodore

Kopfman, 6-14-66. I thought you said your uncle's name was Archie-something."

"Archie-bald. The name on the bracelet is random. It belonged to my uncle in the '60s. He was the one who gave it to me."

"Where's your uncle now?"

"Gone," Martha said sadly.

"Gone where?"

"Gone. Long time passing. Dead."

"Oh. Sorry." I sat on the corner of my bed running my fingers over the name in the bracelet as though Commander Kopfman had been Martha's uncle. I carefully returned Martha's most prized possession. "I didn't mean to upset you. You want to go home now?" I asked softly, hesitatingly.

"No. I'm okay. I just don't like to talk about it very much." Tears filled her green eyes as she pushed brown curls away from her face.

Martha quickly turned her attention to the notebook on my desk that I had started about Miss Janine. Opening it, she read aloud, "Who killed Miss Janine? What's this?"

I tried to get the notebook away from her but Martha held it just out of my reach. "It's just a hobby. I like to solve puzzles. Miss Janine was my friend."

"So you thought you'd find her killer?"

"Well, yeah. You don't have to make it sound so stupid."

"I didn't mean it that way. I guess I don't find puzzles all that interesting." I thought I saw something else in her eyes.

"Let me fill you in on some of the major players in the sixth grade," Martha said, laying the book down. This was my first taste of one of Martha's skills: she changed subjects quickly when she felt insecure.

We sat cross-legged on the window seat, our backs against the walls on either side of the bay window. "Norm Parkey is a huge pain. He'll probably end up President of the United States!" We both laughed at this. "Jeb Seely's a hunk but only interested in sports. His parents run the Warner Inn. Kate Adams is real shy but super-smart. Her brother Mike is year ahead of us."

"And how about Miss Fiddler?" I asked. "She seems too cool to be a teacher. All my teachers in New Jersey were, like, eight thousand years old. I'm sure they went home at night and hung from the ceiling like bats or something."

"She is cool but she's a teacher. Her Dad was Sheriff a long time ago. I've known her all my life. She lives near me."

"Hey! Let's go to your house tomorrow after school. I'd love to see more of Warner with someone who has lived here longer than me!"

Martha hesitated. "Uh, sure, okay. But I'll have to check with my Mom first. Okay, time's up," she said, her turn to change the subject. "Let me see it."

"See what?"

"You know what."

"Don't have a clue."

"Yeah, right. If you don't let me see it, I'll bug you 'til you die. Pull it out."

I knew precisely what she wanted to look at: my hand. I liked Martha's bossy nature. And I needed her. I was also pretty sure, by the way, that a careful examination of the damage to my hand would end this friendship. I took a deep breath, shut my eyes and produced my left hand.

I could feel Martha's hands on my wrist as she turned it this way and that. I steeled myself for the brush off, certain that Martha would be totally grossed out by this time.

"It's no big deal, Kath. Were you born this way or was it an accident?"

"Accident. At least that's what my parents told me. My hand was crushed when I was little and the doctors removed my fingers. Please, please **please** don't talk about it with anybody! It's bad enough being new." I realized too late that I had whined like a baby. I tried to recover. "Are you going to get weird on me and not want to be my friend any more?"

"About this? No way! Have other kids been weird?"

"That's the way some kids acted when I was younger and I guess I haven't forgotten it. They'd see my hand and then turn their faces away like I was some freak or something."

"Then they're too stupid to get it. It wasn't your fault and you shouldn't be dissed for it. It's part of who you are. It doesn't bother me but I can understand why you hide it. There are those out there, not to mention any names like Norm Butthead Parkey, who wouldn't be so cool about it."

I smiled at my new friend and put my hand back in its safe place.

CHAPTER EIGHT

MARTHA AND I SPENT a lot of time together over the next few weeks. She showed me all of the cool places in Warner. One Saturday I called her with a great idea. My recent trip to Janine's Restaurant had given me new information.

"I'll ride over to your house," I said. "We always come here. Give me directions and be real specific. I'm an airhead when it comes to finding places I've never been before." I had expected her to laugh but she didn't.

"Well, it's really not a good time to come over, Kath. I'll ride over to the palace." Martha had taken to calling my house "the palace".

"Why isn't it a good time? It never seems like a good time to go to your house. Why not?"

"Look," she said trying to lighten the mood, "my Mom has been real busy and the house is a mess. My brother Norman is no help. Next time, 'kay?"

I gave in. It seemed like it took Martha forever to get to my house. I waited outside for her to arrive the moment I got off the phone with her. I paced, swung on the glider and then paced some more. I heard her before I saw her: the crunch of gravel under the tires of her Schwinn signaled her arrival. I raced off the porch, almost falling to my knees, and grabbed her by the arm. "You've got to hear this!" I whispered as softly as I could.

"Take it easy!" she warned. "That's the only left arm I have!"

"Sorry. This is really good stuff, though. Let's go up to my room."

Martha followed me through the kitchen and up the back stairs to the second floor hallway. She seemed to dawdle every time she came over to my house. "By the way," Martha said as we continued down the hallway, "this is one of the neatest houses on the island."

"Huh?"

"My Mom cleans rental units for Warner Realty in the summer and she sometimes lets me come with her. I get to see inside these cool houses and dream about my own house someday. She even pays me a buck or two to help out! The more cottages she does, the more money she gets."

"Literally only a buck or two?" I asked.

"No! I was poking fun of that old call collect commercial on TV. It'll save a buck or two?"

I smiled knowing the reference. "Yeah. You watch a lot of TV, huh? But why does she have to clean cottages when she works all day during the week?"

"My brother needs braces and my mom has to save every penny."

"You aren't going to believe what I saw today at Miss Janine's!"

By this time Martha had curled up in my desk chair, lazily twirling around. Her eyes glanced at everything again. "Shell pink paint. I meant to tell you last time. Nice touch. I just can't get this desk out of my head. Can your parents adopt me? Say, Kath, what kind of disposable income do we have here?"

I turned around quickly from the bookshelf where I had been foraging through some papers. My first sense was that this was a rude question but then I realized that I wasn't even sure what she meant. "What?"

"Disposable income. You know, my Mom says that these summer cottage owners have lots of disposable income. I guess that's money you can throw away."

I pulled a Martha and quickly changed the subject. "Listen to this!"

I watched as Martha stopped in mid-spin using her hands on the side of the desk. She then turned enough to prop up her feet and said, "Shoot."

"I went over to the restaurant this morning. I needed to pick up my stuff from class this summer. I heard Mr. Otto and the janitor fighting." I perched myself on the window seat just opposite Martha.

"The janitor? I don't know who cleans at Janine's."

"Not the restaurant janitor. The school janitor. That guy I ran into the first week of school? The one you rescued me from?"

"Oh, Mr. Tucker. What were they fighting about?"

"It sounded like they were fighting over Miss Janine."

She stood and went over to sit on the bed with her back resting against the headboard. "Ooo, nice headboard," she said, as she rubbed her hand over the soft cushiony surface. " I could get **real** used to this!"

"Marth! Would you please stay on task!" I said, mock scolding her like our Spanish teacher at school.

"Okay, okay," she laughed. "What did they say?"

"It sounded like Mr. Otto and the janitor knew each other a long time ago. And the janitor blamed Mr. Otto for Miss Janine's death."

Martha stared into space.

"Well?"

"I'm thinking. I'm thinking."

"And I heard something else. The day Miss Janine died?"

"Go on."

"Well, I overheard Miss Janine and a guy named Connor something-or-other fighting about a recipe. She said that he couldn't read. And he said that she was a thief."

"This is getting good! Kath, we do need to solve this mystery." Martha held up her pinkie and looked at me. "Pinkie swear," she said. I gave her my right pinkie in return and that's when we started our detective agency. "Just like Perry Mason."

"Who's that? A friend of your Mom's?"

Martha laughed about as hard as I had ever seen her laugh. "That's a good one, Kath!"

"What? What did I say?"

"Perry Mason a friend of Carmella's!" I had never heard Martha refer to her mother by anything but her first name.

"Okay, I'll bite. Who is he?"

"He's a character on a TV show from the sixties."

"You know," I said, "I've been meaning to ask you about this thing you have for a decade you weren't even alive in."

Martha stopped giggling and looked away. She had a far-off look in her eye as though she were trying to find the answer herself. "Happiness."

"Whose?"

"Carmella's," Martha said softly.

I let silence fill the space between us, wrapping around us like a warm shawl.

"Okay. Back to our mystery. Do you think any adults will listen to us?"

"We need to go to Oceanside." Martha rubbed her hands together. I watched her do this and, for the first time, I noticed how badly she bit her nails.

"Isn't that a whole 'nother island?" I asked.

"Yeah. But that's where the main Sheriff's Office is." She was quiet for a moment. "Maybe we can get to see the evidence file if it's kept there."

Discussion of evidence in the case of "Who Killed Miss

Janine" reminded me of a juicy tidbit. I grabbed Martha's shoulder when I said, "I saw a body bag!"

"When? You never told me."

"It didn't come up until now."

"When?" she asked and before I could answer she said, "Was Miss Janine in it?"

"I think so. I didn't see it open or anything. It was the day after the fight I told you about. Before school started."

I felt relieved when Martha didn't press me more about the body bag. I think I had stored the information away so I didn't have to deal with it at the time it happened.

"What can we use for our cover?" Martha asked herself. "What else is in Oceanside?" I watched as Martha's eyes scanned the room for inspiration. "The main library. That's it!"

"That's what?"

"Our excuse. We'll say that we have to go over to Oceanside for some school project."

"And then what? Sneak out to the Sheriff's Office? I don't think so, Marth. Some adult would have to take us and they would see us leave the library. And nobody in the Sheriff's Office would talk to little kids." The whine in my voice grew louder like the transmission on some eighteen-wheeler on a bad stretch of road. I really wanted to do it, to solve this mystery, but faced with the reality of actually doing something, I felt paralyzed. I hated being afraid.

"Well, you might be right," she said.

No! Don't back down. Force me to do this! Before I had the chance to open my mouth, Martha cut in.

"Maybe we can see what's up with Mr. Otto and John Tucker. There might be some old newspaper articles or something at the library. And at least we can work on our science projects for school."

CHAPTER NINE

Martha and I sat together at lunch the next day trying to come up with a strategy for our investigation. We spent most of the lunch period watching other students come and go with Martha's keen editorials thrown in.

Norm Parkey strolled over to our table and invited himself to join us. "Hey, girls. Whatcha doin'?"

"Nothing, Parkey," Martha said. "Buzz off."

"What's this?" he asked, snatching away my notebook. I grabbed for it and missed which caused me to fall partway off the bench.

"It's my private stuff, Norm. Give it back!"

"Private stuff? Ooo, private stuff! This should be pretty good, then." He flipped through the few pages of my notes and I noticed that he moved his lips when he read.

"Hey, everybody!"

"Norm, come on," Martha begged.

"Norm, please don't do this," I said, standing to try and get my book back.

"Norm, come on, please don't do this," he said in a mocking tone. I felt my face redden.

Norm Parkey cleared his throat and began to read. "Dear Diary: A few weeks ago I saw the man I think killed Miss

Janine. He was big and mad and seemed to know her quite well. He busted in to the restaurant demanding that she take something off of the menu but I'm not sure what it was. He hurt her by grabbing her around the throat and whispering something that I couldn't hear all of. He saw me and I'm worried that he might hurt me, too."

The lunch area, normally abuzz with noise, was silent. I hung my head so low that my chin practically touched my chest. I looked up when I heard Miss Fiddler walk across the room and saw the furrow in the center of her eyebrows.

"By the way," Norm stage whispered to me, "you misspelled restaurant." The whole school cracked up.

"I'll take that now, Norm," said Miss Fiddler. I breathed in deeply feeling that the most awkward moment of my tiny existence had finally ended.

"And I want to talk with you, Kathy. Now."

Why did she have to say that? Right in front of everybody? I trailed behind Miss Fiddler like a bad puppy. I could feel the looks of disapproval my classmates gave me.

I followed her into an empty classroom. "What is this in your notebook, Kathy? You've obviously had this information for a while. Were you going to tell anyone about it?"

I answered honestly. "Miss Fiddler, it all happened pretty fast and I didn't think about it in terms of its importance until I started thinking more and more about Miss Janine and her death. I couldn't tell you what this guy looked like just that the memory of him scared me."

"Do you remember a name?"

"Connor somebody."

Miss Fiddler nodded her head and said, "Connor Samson. He and Janine went to culinary school together and at one time were boyfriend and girlfriend."

"Does he live near here?"

"No. He lives near Oceanside on Peterson's Isle but his restaurant, The Old Salt, is near here. Did anyone ask you if you knew anything?"

"Yes. The police asked if I was at the restaurant the day she died."

"And what did you tell them?"

"Yes."

"Anything else?"

"They asked if I had seen anything and I was thinking only of whether or not I saw someone kill her. I didn't."

"I've got to tell you, Kathy, I'm disappointed. You have to promise me that if you think of anything else you'll tell me and we'll go see Ray Corcoran. Deal?"

"Deal," I said, thinking of Deputy Ray, the tall, tanned, best-blue-eyes-in-the-galaxy guy I met this past summer at the restaurant.

After school I walked over to Janine's Restaurant. I'm not sure why but I felt drawn to it like a tractor beam had pulled me back there. I wandered into the kitchen garden and gazed at the pots of herbs that Janine had started to teach me about.

I reached out, touched the lavender between my thumb and index finger. I remembered Janine doing that same thing, closing her eyes, smelling its earthy scent. I didn't hear the kitchen's screen door open and close. The next thing I knew, Mr. Otto was standing next to me.

"I always think of Janine when I come out here, out to this space. She loved this garden."

I looked at him and saw how Janine's death had weighed heavily on him. His blue eyes, normally sparkling with amusement, were sad and he looked really tired. Mr. Otto was stocky. Built Ford tough my Dad would say, describing a man who had weight in his hips. "I haven't been back here in the garden since that day," I said. "I miss her."

"I do too."

We sat on a bench in the part of the garden farthest from the kitchen door. I know that sounds like it was acres away but it was only a dozen or so steps beyond the herb garden. Janine had set a country bench back in amongst the trees for a peaceful place to hide from the world. She told me that she liked to hang out there when things in her life were upsetting her or the restaurant was stressful.

And now I chose this place.

"Is everything okay, Kathy?"

I thought carefully about his question. If Miss Janine had asked me I could have answered immediately. I didn't mind confiding in her. But with Mr. Otto?

"You can feel free to talk with me, you know. I know that you and Janine had shared confidences. I did so with her as well."

"How did you and Miss Janine meet?"

Mr. Otto smiled at me. It was a wonderful grin that told a story all its own. "At culinary school."

"Culinary school is cooking school, right?" I asked.

"Yes."

"Were you a student, too?"

"No, no. Far from that," he replied, chuckling. "I was one of the teachers."

"You were?"

"Yup. Taught sauces, soups, that sort of thing."

"Miss Janine was starting to teach me things about cooking."

"Did you like it?"

I swung my legs back and forth under the bench trying to decide whether or not I could tell him what I really thought. I decided that I could. "Not really. Well, not at first. I'm not sure if I liked learning things about cooking or just liked learning from Miss Janine."

I looked at Mr. Otto then and saw him smile a smile of understanding. "Well, if you want to keep learning I'd be happy to try and pick up where she left off."

I nodded my head, which was the kind of answer my mother hated most. A non-answer answer she called it.

"You think about it, then," he said. He didn't seem upset about my non-answer answer.

"Was she a good student?"

"Janine? She could have been the best student we had at the school."

"But?"

"But she wasn't. She and Connor Samson found each other right about then and she fell under his spell." His eyes darkened just a bit as he spoke those words.

"If you're worried about your hand getting in the way, Janine told me what you and she were doing to help strengthen your working paw."

My face must have registered surprise because Mr. Otto smiled and patted my arm.

"Kathy, I'm the one who helped her work on her hand after it was cut."

I felt a mixture of relief and confusion. Relieved that he was the nice person who helped her and confused because he made it sound like what happened to Miss Janine might not have been an ordinary accident.

CHAPTER TEN

WHEN MRS. CUNNINGHAM took Martha and me to the main library in Oceanside the next Saturday morning, it thrilled me that Martha still wanted to be seen with me after the past week's embarrassment in the lunch room. In fact, she didn't seem fazed by it.

Arriving back home, Mrs. Cunningham pulled into our circular drive and cut the engine on her station wagon. Now, this wasn't just any station wagon. This was an old Vista Cruiser. From, you guessed it, the sixties. It had wood paneling on the outside and worn seats that were repaired with duct tape. The back seat where I sat was stacked with everything Mrs. Cunningham might need at any time of day.

"Are you sure it's okay for Martha to stay for dinner, Kathy?" Mrs. Cunningham asked. When she said Martha's name, it came out sounding more like Mawtha.

"Mom!" Martha exclaimed.

"Well, Marty, we don't want to impose on the Harmons. Don't rug me about this."

"Rag, Mom."

"What did I say?"

"Rug. It's rag. Don't rag on me."

I smiled watching the two of them tease each other. They seemed more like sisters than mother and daughter. Mrs.

Cunningham wore lots more make-up than other moms. Martha told me once that she still loved to use that white, frosted lipstick by some English company called Yardley that was so cool in the sixties. And Mrs. Cunningham definitely liked mascara, if you know what I mean. "Whatever. This is a lovely house, Kathy."

"Thanks. Mrs. Cunningham I know my parents would love to meet you and then you could feel better about Martha staying for dinner."

"Oh, she doesn't need to do that, Kath," Martha answered a little too quickly.

"Hey, no big deal. Come on in."

Martha rolled her eyes at me and climbed out of the front seat at the same time her mother did. We all walked into the kitchen together.

"Mom? Dad? I'd like you to meet Martha's mom, Mrs. Cunningham."

My parents were reading different parts of the paper and sitting in overstuffed easy chairs in the nearby family room. They jumped up to meet Mrs. Cunningham, both extending hands at the same time so that she didn't know whose to take first. And then she did the unexpected: she took my parent's hands in both of hers. Everyone laughed. Except Martha.

"Would it be okay if Martha stayed for dinner?" I asked. "Mrs. Cunningham will be out tonight and doesn't want Martha home alone."

"Sure, she's more than welcome any time, Mrs. Cunningham."

"Call me Carmella, please. That would be great. Thanks so much. I'll swing by here and pick her up as soon as I can."

"She's welcome to stay the night if that would be easier for you."

"Well, we'll see. If it gets too late I'll take you up on that."

After Mrs. Cunningham left, Martha said, "Your parents are so cool. Sometimes I wonder about Carmella," Martha said as we both toted heavy book bags filled with science project stuff and other tidbits of information up to my room along with bags of snacks.

"Why?"

"She isn't refined like your parents."

"Does she embarrass you?"

"Sometimes."

"Do you think mine don't embarrass me?"

"They just seem so neat."

"Trust me on this. They do to me what your mom does to you. It just seems different because they aren't your parents. Tell me you didn't notice that they're wearing matching outfits."

"Well…"

"They're into this thing lately. Dressing alike as though they were identical twins. Yuck."

"It's okay. At least your Mom doesn't look like she just stepped out of a commercial from 1965 like Carmella does. What do you think we'll have for dinner?"

"My parents will probably go out for dinner since it's Saturday and all."

"They go out every Saturday?"

"Yeah. They call it date night."

"Oh, gross!"

"Yeah."

"Could we have pizza?"

"Maybe. Let's see what we've got here," I said, referring to the microfilm photocopies we had brought back with us. This was like buried treasure to Martha and me. We had to guard it jealously. We spread the articles out on my bed.

Martha read through some of the pieces and then spoke with a mouthful of chips. "John Tucker's divorce was pretty nasty. Apparently, Mr. Tucker got mad when his wife fell for the local hunk and ran off with him. Their divorce hit the papers because the other guy was an Oceanside celebrity. And guess who the local star was?" Martha didn't wait for me to answer. "Otto von Blumm!"

"Do you think that Mr. Tucker and Mr. Otto are the same people from that article?"

"Honey," she said in mock heavy Southern drawl, "this ain't the big city. You bet! First, Mr. Otto's name is so weird that there could only be one of him in Oceanside. I wish we had phone books from back then to check and see if that were true. But then there's Mr. Tucker."

"But one story said that Mr. Tucker was this genius and now he's cleaning school toilets? Doesn't make sense." I rose from the bed to stretch and think a little. I picked up my yellow kitten, Fuzzhead, and slung her over my shoulder like a sack of potatoes.

Martha looked up, greeted Fuzzhead, and went on. "It would make sense if the whole divorce thing wrecked him and he fell on hard times."

∾

Over a large pepperoni pizza we fished around for more details. Before us on the kitchen table were all of the articles.

"Your Mom must really love to cook," Martha said around a hunk of pepperoni.

"Not my Mom. My Dad. He's constantly ordering kitchen stuff from catalogues," I said, stopping short. We had started our own jigsaw puzzle of sorts on a large piece of newsprint. We cut out all of the things we knew about the mystery, the murder, and the players as far as we knew them. I desperately hoped that something visual would help us out.

"I wonder if detectives do it this way?" asked Martha.

"Sort of. I mean you've seen cop shows where they use

blackboards or erasable boards loaded with information. This is kind of like that only in a way we can work with." I shrugged my shoulders hoping that she wouldn't think that my method was too baby-ish.

"Yeah, I guess. You know, Fiddler's father used to be Sheriff of Warner. We should ask her about...."

"How long ago was that?"

"Before either of us was born."

For the first time that day we were both silent, deep in our own thoughts. Neither of us moved, chewed, breathed loud. I heard nothing but the snick of the battery-operated clock above the sink. "The piece we don't really have yet is where Connor fits in," said Martha.

"And although we have the puzzle pieces we can't say for certain that any of these people killed her. Miss Fiddler asked me if I knew of anything else that happened other than the fight." I cradled my head in my hands hoping that the pressure would force my brain cells to switch on.

"Okay." I wiped pizza grease from my right hand and started to write. "That day we had Miss Janine, Mr. Otto, the produce delivery guy. And Connor." Silence didn't jar any other events from the cobwebs in my head. "Nope. Can't think of anything," I said, shrugging my shoulders.

Martha got up and paced around the kitchen. She found the paper my folks had been reading when we first came in with her mom and said "Courier-Post? Where's that from?"

"Camden County, New Jersey. Home."

"Folks miss the old country, huh?"

"Funny. Ha-ha. Forgot to laugh."

Martha continued to walk around the kitchen as though it was her own. While reading through the paper she poured herself another glass of soda from an open can in the fridge. Then she went over to the desk, picked up my Mom's reading glasses and put them on. She slid them down her nose and peered at me over the top. I knew she was going to break them any minute and it would come out of my allowance.

"Marth, they're my Mom's. If you break them it'll come out of my allowance. She needs them to read. Please take them off." Can you see the big "W" on my back for wuss?

She didn't listen. She continued flipping through the paper and, every so often, would tilt her head back to try to see through the lenses. "Martha, come on!" I begged. It was useless. I tried to pull the glasses off but she ducked. The glasses hit the floor.

And that's what did it. The glasses hitting the floor triggered my memory. "Martha!" I screamed.

"What?" she yelled back, jumping in time with her question.

"Remember when I told you that Connor got physical with Miss Janine? I remember that I picked up a pair of glasses from the floor that didn't belong to her."

"So?"

"So. I wonder whether or not the police found any glasses at the crime scene?"

"Again, so? Maybe the guy picked them up before he left. Or maybe they belonged to someone else who worked at the restaurant."

"No. I know he didn't pick them up before he left because I picked them up from under the lip of the toe kick on the hutch in the dining room. And he had already left. And Miss Janine didn't wear glasses, she wore contacts, and she wouldn't be caught dead in these frames. They were the ugliest things I'd ever seen. Looked like a bad bruise."

"A bruise?"

"Yeah, they were multi-colored plastic frames in purple, yellow, blue, and red. Disgusting," I said, making a face to prove it.

Martha had gone back to reading one of the articles we had copied in the library. She raised her eyebrows and read,

"Local chef Janine McKellum was found dead in her freezer by prep cook Naomi Gilder. Connor Samson, executive chef of The Old Salt Restaurant on Highway 55, said that the community has lost a treasure."

"Connor Samson. This must be the weird name murder club or something." We stood in the middle of the kitchen near the island as the last rays of sunset filtered through a low-lying cloud. Martha's face turned pink-orange. "So if Connor was the one who lost the glasses and no glasses are listed on the crime scene evidence list, it looks like Connor is our guy!" Martha said positively.

We high-fived our cleverness and ran back upstairs.

CHAPTER ELEVEN

L OOK, KATH," MARTHA SAID, "you know where Mr. Otto lives, right?"

"Right," I said hesitantly.

"And you know that he never locks his door, am I right again?"

"Yep. Right again." My steps began to slow in order to delay the inevitable.

"We know he's not home because we swung by the restaurant and saw him working. Right?"

"Mmm hmm."

"And we need to get some more info on Mr. Otto and Miss Janine and this Connor character."

"Yes."

"The only way we'll be able to do that without some adult getting suspicious and then telling us to keep our noses out of it is to go after it ourselves. Sneaky like."

I nodded my head but my heart wasn't in it. Yes I knew that Mr. Otto didn't lock his door. I knew that because when I helped out at the restaurant he sent me to his apartment to get him some medicine that he had forgotten. I felt weird just walking into his place without him being there but he didn't seem to mind one bit. He said that there was nothing to steal and if someone wanted it that badly they could go ahead and take it. I recall telling Martha that part too.

We got to the converted garage where Mr. Otto's apartment was, propped our bikes against a shed and looked up the steps leading to the landing outside his door. Wind chimes tinkled in the breeze. Two white plastic chairs sat to one side. It was late afternoon and this side of the building was in deep shade. We looked around thoroughly before climbing the first step.

"I hate this tacky white plastic furniture," Martha whispered as we got to the top of the stairs. "Oh, and great wind chimes. They look moldy."

"It's called verdigris, I think," I said, trying to call into my mind the term my mother had used for something that had the same color. I had to agree with Martha on this one. They did look moldy.

Once inside, we waited until our eyes grew accustomed to the dark before taking another step. "Do you remember the layout of his place at all?" Martha asked.

"Not really. I was only here once and only went into the bathroom to get his medication."

"Meds, huh?" she asked trying to sound hip. "What'd he need them for?"

"Don't remember." I actually remembered quite well as I was concerned when I saw that it was a vial of nitroglycerine. My grandpa used that for his heart condition.

Finally, the outline of the room took shape. A sofa and table sat to our left with a small square dining table straight ahead. We walked forward cautiously and then Martha turned on a light.

"Hey! Turn that thing off," I said, startled.

"We're not going to get anywhere in the dark. Besides, take a look at those curtains."

I turned and saw where she was pointing. Heavy curtains in a gross gold, green and crimson floral print covered what appeared to be the only window. They reminded me of my grandma's house in the Italian section of Philadelphia. Mr. Otto's couch had the outline of a human shape to it. Dented cushions were done in the same color gold as the drapes. The material tried to look rich and expensive but didn't cut it.

"Hey, Kath, come here."

I walked down the small hallway and into a tiny bedroom. It had a cot-sized bed in it and a stand-alone closet. Martha was already poking her nose into the closet and then into the bathroom. I heard the sound of papers being flipped.

"Martha, come on. How would you like Mr. Otto to break in on your privacy? This isn't right."

"Ah. Yes. Here we are."

"What?"

She had turned on a light and sat on the floor with her back against the cot. She had a piece of paper in her hand.

"What is it?" I asked, sitting next to her.

"A birth certificate."

"Yeah. So?"

"Janine's birth certificate."

That phrase hung in the air for a while. "Why would Mr. Otto have Miss Janine's birth certificate?"

"Maybe because he is her father?" Martha said, more as a statement than a question.

"No way. I think he has her personal stuff. Maybe he cleaned out her place after she died."

"Well, the father's name isn't stated." She held the piece of paper out to me and I looked at the box where the father's name went and saw the word "unknown".

"It doesn't say that he's her father, doofus. It says unknown."

"Who would put it that way if you were proud of who the dad was? Mom must have been trying to hide the father's identity."

"You watch way too much TV," I said, shaking my head. "I still think it's a coincidence. Not everything is weird. C'mon Marth. Let's go. We're not going to find anything here."

Just as I got to the front door Martha went in another direction. I rolled my eyes and sighed.

"Oh keep your socks on," Martha said. "Oh boy. Oh boy!"

"What now?"

Martha stepped over to me with something in her hand. We had turned out the lights so I couldn't see what it was.

"What is it?"

"Let's go," she said, pushing me out the front door and down the steps.

"What?"

"Just ride and I'll show you in a minute."

We pedaled quickly through the village of Warner and out to one of the deserted fishing piers. Martha had a wild look in her eyes.

"One minute you want to go through his place with a microscope and the next you're shoving me out the door. What is going on Martha Cunningham?"

"This." She produced the object from her jacket pocket. It was a pair of glasses with frames the color of a bruise.

∽

Martha and I decided to talk later. I watched as she rode away from me toward a new cluster of homes. I decided then and there to solve the mystery of why Martha did not want me to see her house.

I rode behind her far enough so that I could barely see her. She wheeled around a corner that looked as though it led to a nice house. As I rounded the same corner, I saw that the dirt path led to another cluster of homes.

In a trailer park.

CHAPTER TWELVE

TWO WEEKS AFTER OUR first trip to Oceanside, Martha and I rode the ferry again. "This is the best part of the whole trip. Don't you love this?" Martha asked.

"It's okay," I said. She made me mad and the pitch of the waves made me queasy. Why did Martha Cunningham make me mad? Because.

Because she took that pair of glasses from Mr. Otto's apartment and then wouldn't hang on to them. She forced them into my jacket pocket before we split up saying that they would be safer with me because I didn't have brothers.

I felt guilty enough for going into Mr. Otto's apartment without his say so and then felt worse that Martha had stolen something. Maybe being friends with her wasn't such a hot idea. And then I remembered.

She was my only friend.

"Okay? Just okay? I love being out here on the water, watching the gulls trail behind the boat, people throwing crackers and bits of bread for them. Every once in a while, a big gull will sit high up on the roof of the control tower and squawk. I love the feel of the wind in my hair!" Martha spread her arms wide and closed her eyes. I watched the wind lift bangs off of her forehead.

I tried to convince myself that I had to stop being such a weenie all of the time and get some backbone. I had started this adventure and I should finish it! Yes, we had lied to our parents. Again. This time I told my mother that I was at Martha's house and she told her mom the same. That's how we came to be on the Warner ferry going to Oceanside by ourselves. No one looked at us funny. Island kids did this all the time Martha said. And Martha assured me that we would be back home by mid-afternoon.

Our first stop was the Oceanside Sheriff's station. "We'll check what we think happened against the evidence list. Maybe we can even see the crime scene photos!" Martha exclaimed.

That thought turned my stomach even further. Leave out the blood, guts and gore. Go ahead and call me a wuss.

What really bothered me about seeing the crime scene photos was the possibility that I might have to look at my dead friend. I wanted to remember her the way she was when she was alive. I thought going to a funeral home to view a body was disgusting enough. This would be even worse.

Inside the Sheriff's station a short, thin man stood behind the counter wearing the familiar brown uniform.

"Hi," Martha said.

"Hello. May I help you with something? Lost cat?" He smirked at us.

"No. No lost cat," Martha answered. "We'd like to see a file, please."

"A file?"

"Yes. Yes, sir."

"Is it a pending investigation?" The smirk was growing.

"Yes it is. I'd like to see the evidence list and crime scene photos."

Then he laughed. Not a polite little chuckle but a full-scale belly-holding laugh.

"What's so funny, Officer?" Martha asked in her best adult voice.

"I didn't know we had deputized a pair of little girls!" Tears were beginning to run down his face. If he thought this situation was that funny he must lead a pretty boring life.

"Hey! Come on," Martha said, with a trace of whine in her voice. "Are you going to let us see this stuff or not?"

"Nancy Drew wants to see the file! Hey, Lou! Come see the little girl de-tectives!" the Deputy shouted as he disappeared into a back room. I could still hear him laughing.

"Come on, Martha," I said, tugging on the sleeve of her sweater. "Let's go. He can't seem to stop laughing long enough to listen."

We sat down on a bench outside the station. I looked at my friend and saw that she was crying. "Hey, Martha, it's okay. He's just some dummy. Forget him."

"He makes me so mad!" Tears left trails down her cheeks. "Why do adults treat kids like that? He made me feel like I was stupid or something. Like, because I'm a kid I don't have anywhere near his sense or brains. And then," Martha continued between hitched sobs, "then I get mad at myself for crying over some moron. I hate it when I get so mad that I cry."

I draped my arm around her shoulder. "I know how you feel." We sat there until Martha had calmed down. "Besides, guys like Deputy Dawg back there are too dumb to know quality when they see it." This was the first time I felt that I could help Martha instead of the other way around. And the first time that I had seen Martha's vulnerability.

"I'm not stupid," she mumbled.

"No, you're not. And neither am I. Now, since we can't get a look at that file, let's work on it a different way."

CHAPTER THIRTEEN

MARTHA FOUND CONNOR SAMSON'S address in the phone book so we pedaled over to a large one-story house with lots of trees and shrubs. In case you're wondering, I taught myself to ride one-handed pretty well. I can even ride with no hands and just balance the bike with the weight of my body.

We left our bikes leaning against a tree out of view. "Boy, he must have some bucks," Martha said.

"Why? It looks pretty average. Nothing to write home about."

"See all the trees and bushes and junk? They look pretty healthy, right? It takes water to do that, my friend. This is an island. Carmella says that water is priceless."

We walked around the outside of the house trying to find anything that could prove our theory that this guy was the killer. We looked under bushes, in the mailbox, peeked into the garage through a window. Nothing.

On our second trip around the yard I whispered to Martha, "What are we looking for anyway? I mean, it isn't like he's going to have a sign saying this way to the murder weapon." Just as Martha started to answer, the back door opened.

"Can I help you two?" The voice, low and resonant,

seemed to have a slight accent. British. I looked at the man who had fought with my friend and thought he was such a phony. He was no more British than my Aunt Clara from Cleveland.

I noticed a few more details about him this time around. His hair, now streaked white-blond, stood in spikes on top of his head. Khaki shorts and a white shirt with sleeves rolled above his elbows showed off a dark tan.

Martha found her voice before me. "Have you seen my puppy, Mister? He's black and tan and just a little guy? He's lost and I miss him!" she cried in her best little girl voice. Man, she should get an Oscar for this.

"No. Haven't seen a pup around. What's his name?"

"Navy. His name's Navy." I eyed Martha. Navy? What loony would call her puppy Navy?

"Well, if I see *Navy*," he continued, "I'll let you know. Where do you live?"

"A couple blocks down. On Morton. Okay if I come back and check with you again?"

"Sure, sure," he said almost tenderly. "I'll keep an eye out." I was pretty certain that he didn't care about some girl's lost puppy. I remembered his practically strangling Miss Janine. He'd probably kick a stray pup to the moon.

As we left his yard and collected our bikes, Martha started to call out the imaginary pup's name. I chimed in to make it look real. Not until we were back down the street and away from the house did I speak in a normal tone.

"Navy? You'd call a puppy Navy?"

"It was the first thing that came to mind. I thought of the dog in those Old Navy commercials and, well, you know the rest."

"Why did you ask to come back and check with him?"

"Since I don't live on Morton, which **is** a real street in the neighborhood by the way, I didn't want him asking for a phone number or anything."

"Good thinking, partner!" I said clapping her on the back. "Did you happen to see what was hanging around his neck?"

We stopped our bikes. Martha stood with one foot on the road and the other on a pedal.

"The glasses," I said. "They're the same ones I saw in the restaurant and the same ones you took from Mr. Otto's place."

We sat on benches outside a local store eating animal crackers and drinking sodas. "Why," I said with a mouthful of elephants, "do you think there are so many pairs of glasses with the same frames?"

Martha held up a finger, signaling that she couldn't talk yet. She swallowed and began. "I was thinking that same thing. We have two pairs so far, right?"

"Right. The ones you took from Mr. Otto's, which, by the way, I'm still mad at you about."

"Why?"

"Because they don't belong to us, they're Mr. Otto's...."

"Or Miss Janine's."

"No. I told you. She wore contact lenses."

"That doesn't mean that she had them in all the time. I know people who wear contacts during the day but glasses when they're home. Or maybe she used 'em to read."

"Okay. You've got a point there," I said, conceding. "Then we have the pair that I just saw hanging around Connor's neck."

"Are you sure," she said taking a swig of her drink, "that they're the same frames?"

"Pretty sure."

When we were through with our feast we rode down to the ferry. I noticed a lot of cars going back toward Oceanside. When we got down to the dock we found out why.

"Sorry guys," said a ferry worker. "Ferry isn't running this afternoon. Storm's about to hit," he said, pointing upward. Martha and I tilted our heads back to gaze at the darkening sky. The wind suddenly picked up and rain began. A bolt of lightning and corresponding thunder backed up the threat.

CHAPTER FOURTEEN

WATER POURED FROM THE SKY like a plane dusting crops. We were soaked to the skin in minutes. Martha and I ran onto the porch of the nearby Visitor's Center. I was not a happy camper. My unhappiness existed for a number of reasons: first, I was wet; second, I was going to be late and couldn't even call my Mother to tell her where I was because, third; I had lied. Again.

"Wow! What a storm! Isn't this great?" Martha asked as she shook water droplets off her curly head like a dog.

"No. It's not great. We're stuck here. It's getting late and we're not going to get home in time to back up our excuses. I hate this!" I screamed, stomping away from her.

"You haven't lived here very long," Martha said. "These storms come up fast and leave just as fast. I bet we're out of here within the hour." She tried to be comforting but I didn't take it that way. I took it as a slap in the face that I wasn't a native. Big fat deal. I shrugged her off. We'd better be out of here within the hour. Or else. Or else what? I'm on an island away from home. What am I going to do? I was stuck.

The hour came and went and so did the next. Darkness ended the afternoon and my hopes of getting home.

"We can't stay here at the Visitor's Center overnight," Martha said. "We need to find someplace to bunk."

Martha mused over this while I fumed. My anger increased with each of her silly words. Bunk. Yeah, that's what this is. Bunk. I cannot believe that Martha hadn't thought about something like this happening. She should have had some kind of plan. Did I have to do all of the thinking for both of us? Now I'm going to be in such huge amounts of trouble that I won't be let out of the house until next summer.

"Why didn't you think of something like this happening?" I blurted out.

Martha whirled around to face me. "What? What do you mean by that? What do I look like, the weather girl?"

"I just think you should have thought of this and had us to the ferry sooner, that's all."

"Oh, I see. Like I'm the only one on this adventure. You started this whole "Who Killed Miss Janine" thing. **You** dragged **me** into this! Do you want me to refund the cost of your lunch too? Why didn't **you** think of this?"

"I just moved here, remember?" Then I did the only adult thing I could think of to do: I turned my back on her.

Several seconds went by in silence. It seemed more like minutes had passed but I knew that was impossible. Martha spoke first.

"Look, Kath, I don't like this any better than you do but we have to deal with the situation. We're stuck here for the night. Let's work together to find a safe place to stay instead of fighting. Okay?"

Her last word came out thin and weak as though afraid of my answer. I couldn't afford to stay mad at her. I needed her knowledge of Oceanside to get us someplace safe and dry.

"Is there anything I can help with, girls?" Connor Samson's familiar voice came from behind us. It shocked me. He was the last person I had expected to see again so soon.

"What are you doing at the ferry in weather like this?" Connor asked. "Are you by yourselves?"

We stared at him.

"No. No," I said, this time being the first to find my voice. "We're still looking for my friend's pup, Navy." This time Martha gave me the eye.

"Tell you what I think," Connor said. "I don't think there is a pup. I think you were being sneaky and nosy. What are you two so curious about?"

I wanted to answer by telling him that I was curious about why he murdered my friend and that I thought he had the worst taste in glasses frames that I had ever seen but, well, I valued my short little life. He interrupted my thoughts.

"I **do** recognize you now," he said looking at me. "You're the little girl I saw at Janine's the last time we were together."

That tore it. I hated being called little girl but it made me madder to hear him try to suggest that the last time he saw Janine they were friends who had gotten together for a chat.

I looked into his eyes and saw nothing. No emotion, just emptiness. "You mean the day she died?" I asked in the sweetest voice I could muster at the time.

"Yes. I guess that would have been the day."

Guess my butt. He knew darn well it was the day.

"We've got to go now, Mister," Martha said trying to back both of us out of the situation. She hooked her arm through mine. My relief at her intervention lessened my temper.

"I'd like to talk with you two some more," he said, following us into the Visitor Center.

"We've gotta ditch him," Martha whispered in my ear.

"No kidding. He makes me nervous."

Luck was with us for what seemed like the first time that day. As Connor walked in behind us someone called out his name. When he turned to see who had called to him, we pivoted back through the door and out to the safety of our bikes.

I rode as fast as I could in the rain and wind behind Martha. Even though I used both hands, she was clearly the better rider especially in weather like this. We pedaled back to Oceanside from the ferry and I felt safe as long as I kept her rear reflector in my sight. Martha knew this place far better than I did. She had mentioned going to find her mother's best friend, Sara, and I prayed that she could help us.

"This is scary," I said, trying to talk myself into feeling better about everything. It didn't help. Cars continued to race by us. Spray from car tires licked my face.

The rain didn't let up. I didn't recognize much from this morning and the wind-blown rain made it almost impossible to see anything.

It happened in a split second. I lost it and fell hard to the pavement. A car coming toward me had its bright lights on and I was blinded. A car behind me honked its horn just as I slid-out on sand that had washed across the road.

"Martha!" I screamed, gripping my knee. I could feel something warm coming through my fingers. My butt was planted firmly in a pothole, my feet tangled in the bike's pedals.

Bright lights from behind me got brighter and I could hear the low rumble of a car idling in neutral. A car door opened.

I was trapped.

CHAPTER FIFTEEN

I CLOSED MY EYES AND WAITED. I knew that I couldn't get up fast enough and certainly couldn't run. I hoped that the driver behind me had stopped to help. And that it wasn't Connor Samson.

"Oh, Kath, I'm so sorry!" Martha said, finding me on the ground in a pool of wet sand and tears. I didn't want her to see me crying but my knee hurt badly. "I turned around to make sure you were still behind me and you weren't anywhere to be seen! This is all my fault!" she exclaimed, half in tears herself.

In that instant, the driver who had stopped behind me had returned to the car and drove off down the road. I looked up in time to see a bit of the rear license plate.

"Who was that?" Martha asked.

"Don't know. Somebody honked a horn behind me and that's when I lost it. I hurt my knee."

"Stay here. I'll be right back."

She trotted in the direction of the Sheriff's station that I could see was maybe a hundred or so yards away. I wanted to ask her not to leave me, to stay with me because my panic and embarrassment were growing but she had gone before I could say these things. After I thought about it for a minute, I was glad that I hadn't opened my big mouth. I would have looked like an even bigger baby. And I didn't want anyone to know that I needed my Mom so bad right then I could have screamed.

Martha returned shortly with Deputy Ray Corcoran. Great! The guy I thought was so cute would see me in this tangled mess with a soggy butt.

"Hey, there. Let me help," he said, untangling my feet and picking me up in his arms. Maybe this wasn't so bad after all. I rested my head against his strong shoulder like I used to do with my Dad. Martha pushed both bikes to the Sheriff's station.

The station was warm and comforting. I couldn't wait to get into some dry clothes and curl up under a toasty blanket. I wasn't ready for Deputy Ray to let me go yet either.

"That deputy's probably still laughing at me back there," Martha whispered to me. I smiled.

Ray set me down on a chair and examined my torn knee. "Doesn't look too bad. Just scraped is all. I'll get the first aid kit."

"He's kind of cute," I blurted out to my friend. "I met him over the summer but I don't think he remembers me," I said, finishing just before Ray reappeared.

"You're blushing, Kath. Got a crush on ol' Deppity Ray?"

"No I don't, Martha Cunningham," I responded quickly before he could overhear.

"Okay," he said, smiling just a bit too broadly. "So getting to know more people in Warner?" he asked as he dug out bandages and antibiotic ointment.

I watched him work on my knee. I noticed that his short hair was starting to turn gray and I thought the blue of his eyes was the color of the sky after a rain storm. "You remember me?"

"Sure. Pretty lady like you, new in town. I remember."

Behind him Martha pretended to stick her finger down

her throat and gag. I stuck my tongue out at her.

"So, Martha Cunningham. What're you doing over here? Your Mom with you?"

"I could ask you the same thing, Mr. Deputy-soon-to-be-head-of-the-Sheriff's-Department-in-Warner."

"Smarty," he said, sticking out his tongue at her. "Really, Martha. Are you here alone?"

Martha continued to avoid the question by asking him, "Are you?"

"I'm here filling in for one of the guy's who's out sick. What's your excuse?"

"Boy, I sure was glad to see you," I said, jumping in and trying to divert the subject away from the fact that we were here alone. "You know each other?"

"Since I was little," Martha said.

"Mart? Your Mom here?" he asked again.

"No," she replied softly. "Hey, Ray. Somebody did this to Kathy on purpose. Tell him, Kat." That was the first time anyone had called me by the nickname I liked best.

"Is that true?" he asked. I looked deeply into his eyes.

"I'm not sure. I was riding behind Martha and someone honked a horn right behind me. That's when I fell."

"And when I rode back to her the driver was out of the car and coming toward her and—." Martha stopped short when she realized that she had said too much.

"And what?" Ray asked.

Silence filled the room.

"And then what? Kathy? Do you know who it was?"

"I'm only guessing but we had some words with Connor Samson at the Visitors Center."

"Connor? What was said?"

"He recognized me from Janine's Restaurant the day she died."

"You never mentioned that," he said.

I shrugged. I really didn't want to go any further with

this. Not right now. "I didn't know it was important. He and Janine had a big fight."

Ray stood and got a pad of paper to write on. "Tell me what happened."

I took a deep breath, looked at Martha, and she nodded at me. I related the events of that afternoon including Connor's threats to Janine.

"Are you sure it was Connor behind you tonight?"

"No."

"Did you see any part of a license plate?"

"Yes. Let me think," I said chewing on a thumbnail. "Impossible Chief?"

Ray smiled and said, "Imperial Chef. He has a vanity plate that says IMPLCHF. Was that it?"

"Yeah, that's it. I saw it for just a second but I think that's it."

"That's Connor." He paused long enough to finally take stock of two drenched kids. "Say. You guys must be freezing. Want some hot chocolate?"

"Yes please," I said, answering first to get my polite young lady points in before Martha.

"Oh, brother," she replied, rolling her eyes in my direction.

"So what were you guys doing in Oceanside without parents?" Ray asked, repeating his initial questioning of Martha. He put away the first aid kit and led us into the kitchen.

"Got stuck after doing some research at the library," Martha said. I eyed her for the second time that day.

"Really," Ray said suspiciously. "Well, what are we going to do with you tonight? Ferry's not running again 'til morning. First thing we need to do is call some parents I would imagine. Let them know you're okay. I'm on night duty tonight and we're not full. You could sleep on cots." Relief flooded over me as he handed us dry clothes.

"I don't want to take your spare set of clothes," I said.

"That's okay. I keep sweatshirts and shorts here in case of emergencies. I think this qualifies." I clutched his clothes to me as he showed us to the ladies locker room.

"Want some pizza?" he asked.

"Thin crust. No anchovies," Martha ordered over her shoulder as we went in to change.

CHAPTER SIXTEEN

T HE FOLLOWING AFTERNOON I snuck out of the house to meet Martha at the Community Store even though I was grounded for the rest of my miserable little life. I surprised myself by doing this. I have always been a good girl, always counted on to do the right thing. Now rebellious, I rode my bike away from my house and down the dirt lane.

We sat in rockers on the porch eating Drumsticks and watched sailboats as they drifted on the breeze out of Pirate Harbor into Warner Bay and beyond. Their crisp white sails stood out against the deep blue sky.

"Do you still miss New Jersey with a view like this?" Martha asked.

"Well, yeah, I still miss going to the Cherry Hill Mall, bowling at PlayDrome, that sort of thing," I responded, wiping ice cream from my chin. "But this is pretty awesome, huh?"

"Touristas pay big bucks for this!"

"Touristas?"

"It's Spanish for tourists. Carmella says so. So what happened when you got home?" Martha asked.

"I'm grounded indefinitely and I'm not supposed to talk to you. My parents think you're a bad influence. You?"

"You moved here from New Jersey and **I'm** a bad influence? Gimme a break. Well. Carmella grounded me but then told me that I was a good kid for going to Deputy Ray. But then I got in trouble again because I got you hurt."

"You didn't get me hurt. I got hurt because some moron scared the willies out of me and I was riding in bad weather. So what do we do now?" I didn't really want more of her theories and chance taking but still wanted to solve the mystery. At the end of the day, as Mom would say, Janine was still dead and we didn't have a clue as to why or who did it.

"Unfortunately I think we need to get more adults involved. Nobody's going to listen to us."

"Yeah, well, I tried to tell you that skatey-eight gajillion times, Marth."

"You still have the glasses?"

"Don't start with me! I didn't take them to begin with and then you made me hang on to them for you."

"Whiner. Do you?"

"Yes."

"Where?"

"They're safe."

"Where?"

"Why?"

"Cause I want to know."

"No. You gave them to me for safekeeping. Leave it at that." The glasses were in the bottom of my blanket chest at the end of my bed but I didn't want Martha to know that right now.

"Which adult do you want to go to?" I asked, changing the subject.

"Don't laugh, okay? I think we should go see Fiddler. She's pretty cool and her Dad was Sheriff a long time ago. I think she would listen."

I thought that was one of the more sane decisions Martha had made in this whole adventure.

CHAPTER SEVENTEEN

TWO MONTHS AGO I would have thought it was really weird to know where a teacher lived. I didn't want to know anything about their lives after school even though we all wondered how messy a teacher's house might be. Teachers didn't have lives. They taught.

I could hear the sounds of a football game on TV as we walked up the pathway between flowerbeds. Miss Fiddler's house looked like a cottage, dark gray with maroon trim and shutters. She had lots of flowers and a white picket fence. June, Ward and The Beave would love it here.

"You idiot!" Miss Fiddler's voice traveled through an open window. "Didn't they teach you football in college?"

"Bad call, ref!" said a male voice that sounded like Deputy Ray's.

"No way! The guy has been off sides twice now. In the same play!"

"No, no, no. Bad call."

"Yes, yes, yes. Good call, Ray." Miss Fiddler opened the door to our knock and said, "Hey, guys. How are you doing?"

"We're okay, Miss Fiddler," Martha said. "Is this a bad time to visit?"

"No. No. Ray and I were just arguing over a GOOD call in a football game. What's up?"

"Can we talk to you?"

"Sure."

Miss Fiddler invited us into her living room with a sweep of her arm. It was surprisingly tidy. I honestly didn't know what I expected but I loved her house from the instant I saw it. It was small and neat. Deputy Ray and a black Lab were sprawled on the floor in front of the TV.

"Hey again, girls," Ray said. "This is Jake," he said as the dog sniffed us up and down. After losing interest he went back to his spot beside Ray.

"Kathy, Martha, you know Deputy Corcoran of the Sheriff's Department don't you?"

"Hi, Deputy Corcoran," Martha said sweetly. I inwardly rolled my eyes at her and smiled at him. He did have the cutest blue eyes.

"Good to see you back in Warner, girls," he said.

"What does that mean?" Miss Fiddler asked.

"I ran into the girls in Oceanside yesterday. Research at the library, wasn't it?" He had a cute dimple in his left cheek when he smiled.

౼

An hour and two glasses of lemonade later we finished our story complete with why we were in Oceanside yesterday. Ray ran over to the Sheriff's station and returned with the case file. We finally saw what we had hoped to see in Oceanside.

"Aren't all of the files kept in the main office in Oceanside?" I asked.

"No. Only those files having to do with Oceanside crimes."

"Oh," I said, trying not to be angry about the wasted trip and being grounded. We didn't even have to leave Warner yesterday to see what we'd gone there for.

"There aren't any glasses on the evidence list," Ray said. "I think you have a good theory about them though."

"You do?" Martha asked.

"Yeah. It's a good thought. Now we just have to back it up with some hard evidence. But it's the first break we've had."

"May I see the crime scene pictures?" I asked. "Not the gory ones but the ones of the kitchen?"

Ray passed them to me and he and Miss Fiddler watched while I flipped through them. I felt important. I liked it.

"Hmm. Nope. I thought if I looked at them something would come to me but it didn't. I'm sorry."

"No need to apologize," Ray said. "You two have done good work."

"Even if you did take some pretty big chances," Miss Fiddler said. "I don't like the thought of you two going over to Oceanside alone and then going to Connor Samson's house."

"Yes, we've already gotten the lecture, Miss Fiddler," Martha said. I thought Martha was a little too short with her.

Miss Fiddler's kitchen was cool, too. The color scheme was just like that old show on TV, Happy Days: sun yellow and aquamarine blue with a black and white tile floor. When I placed my empty glass in the sink, I spotted a heavy meat tenderizer on the counter. "Wait a sec!" I yelled. "Deputy, can I see those kitchen photos again?" I said, returning to the living room. Seconds passed before I spoke again. "That's it."

"What's it?" the three said in unison.

"It's what **isn't** there." I grinned, knowing for sure that I had the answer.

"You gonna make us beg or what, Kat?" Martha asked.

"Miss Janine let me use an old meat tenderizer when I took her cooking classes."

"What's your point?" Martha asked.

"It isn't in the photos. It's missing."

"You sure?" Miss Fiddler asked. "I think the Sheriff's Department went all over that kitchen and nobody said anything about a missing meat tenderizer."

"That's right. Because it was old and no one used it but me. I put it in a special place in the center well between the counters, out of the way. It's not there."

"Why a tenderizer? And why just you?" Ray asked.

I remained silent.

"I need a reason for coming up with the tenderizer idea and it would help if you would tell me why."

Terrific. I was about to tell the guy I had a major crush on that I was disfigured. That surely would end any chances for me. I mean I know I'm too young and all but now he probably won't ever speak to me again after seeing my hand. It took all I had to control my tears.

"I have a disability. Miss Janine tried to help me." Everyone waited for me to say more. "I lost the fingers on my left hand when I was a kid," I said, removing my left hand from its hiding spot. I let them look for a moment and then quickly tucked it back in my shorts pocket.

"So that's why you keep your hand in your pocket," Miss Fiddler said. "No problem. Our lips are sealed. Right Ray?"

"Right," he said, looking at me with too much pity. "So what did the tenderizer do for you?"

"Miss Janine was trying to strengthen my right arm so I didn't have to use my left hand as much. She tried to help me find different ways to do things."

"She was cool," Miss Fiddler said.

We were all silent for a moment in remembrance of Janine McKellum.

"This is good, this is good," Ray said. "Thanks for telling us, Kat. Now we have two pieces of evidence. We think Connor has the glasses. If he has the tenderizer too, we're in."

He called me by my favorite nickname! My heart flipped over. But **I** have the glasses. I didn't tell him that part because I wasn't sure how to explain how I came to have a pair of them in my blanket chest. I'm equally not sure about why there were so many pairs of them floating around. I decided not to say anything until I had better answers.

CHAPTER EIGHTEEN

"OH, NUTS," MISS FIDDLER SAID as her overhead projector marker ran out of ink. We had been right in the middle of a lively discussion of the word 'brave' in the book *Downriver*. I was disappointed when she had to stop.

"Okay guys, calm it down. Guys!" she said loudly. The noise level dropped instantly at the sound of her raised voice.

"I'm out of ink. We need to take a break. Would someone please run down to the office and get a new pack of markers? Kathy, how about you?"

"Sure," I said, feeling important. Seeing Miss Fiddler at her house helped me feel less out of place.

Walking down to the office I could hear the sounds of other classes working. Warner School taught students from kindergarten through twelfth grade. As I walked by each classroom, that noise sounded like tuning a radio to find a good station.

The office was in the middle of the main hall where it could be reached by entering the school from either Back Road or Warner School Road. I stood at the counter and didn't see Mrs. Graves, the school secretary but I could see a steaming cup of coffee on the desk and felt like a detective noticing each little detail.

A minute passed and no one appeared so I called out, "Hello? Anyone home?"

"Just a sec," came a man's voice from an office to my right. John Tucker came out.

"Oh!" I said. Seeing this large man up close again made me nervous. "Uh," I stammered, unable to find my voice or train of thought.

"Something I can do for you?"

"Yes. Miss Fiddler asked me to get another pack of overhead projector markers?" He glared at me. "Please?"

John Tucker smirked. It wasn't a smile or a grin. It was a condescending smirk. As he bent down to retrieve the markers I saw a pair of glasses swinging from a strap around his neck. They looked like the same ones that Connor Samson had and the ones I had stashed away in my blanket chest. I couldn't breathe!

"Here we go. Hey. You okay?"

I exhaled, inhaled and smiled, saying the first thing that came to me. "Uh, sure. Just practicing holding my breath is all. Apple bobbing for Halloween!"

Mr. Tucker gave me the markers and I left as quickly as I could. It's a good thing Martha wasn't here or she'd have one up on me for teasing her about calling a puppy Navy. Apple bobbing? Yeah, that's good.

When I got back to class, Miss Fiddler said, "About time. Did you go for a coffee while you were out?"

"Latte. Half caf. Chocolate shavings," Norm Parkey said before I could answer.

The room erupted in laughter and I played along while my mind was racing ahead trying to figure out why Mr. Tucker would have those glasses. And what did it do to our theory about Connor Samson being the killer?

At lunch Martha and I sat at one of the outside tables watching our class play the seventh graders in volleyball.

"Is your knee any better?" Martha asked.

"Yeah."

"Bet you wanted Deppity Ray to change your bandage, huh?"

"No! Well. Maybe," I admitted with a grin.

"So where do we go with our mystery?"

"I think this Connor guy did it but something weird happened at the office this morning when I went to get the overhead markers." Just at that second I spotted Miss Fiddler and called out to her. "Miss Fiddler? Can we talk to you? In private?"

"Sure," she said as she lobbed her lunch sack into a nearby trashcan. "Two points," she said to herself. "Would have been three if I'd made it from the bike rack," she said to us over one shoulder. Martha and I rolled our eyes at each other. Grown-ups.

After checking to see if anyone was in the teacher's lounge, Miss Fiddler signaled us to go in.

"Wow," Martha said. "I've always wanted to know what was back here."

The room was small, furnished with comfortable chairs and an old sofa. A coffee maker was on a counter against one wall, a refrigerator against the other. The room had no windows.

"We come in here to lick the wounds you students rip into us," Miss Fiddler said.

"Yeah, right, Miss Fiddler," Martha said.

"What's up, girls?"

"I saw something in the office today," I said. "When I went to get the markers?" I could hear the soft ticking of a clock, which corresponded with the beating of my heart. "It took me so long because Mrs. Graves wasn't at her desk."

"She's out sick today."

"Oh. Well, this is probably going to sound strange but the janitor was back there in some room."

"Not strange," Miss Fiddler said as she nodded at me. "Mr. Tucker works on our computers and fills in when Mrs. Graves is out. He's kind of all purpose."

Miss Fiddler and Martha were staring at me, urging me to continue. "Well, he came out and I asked for the markers. Just as he bent down to look under the counter I saw them!"

"Saw what?" they said together.

"The glasses! The same glasses that Connor Samson had on when we were snooping around his house. The same ones I remember from the restaurant," I said, gesturing with both hands.

"The exact same ones?" Martha asked. "Are you sure?"

"Yeah. Sure. They're hard to forget."

Miss Fiddler held up her hand. I noticed that she wore a braided black leather bracelet. "Wait guys. Hang on. Since we had our discussion, Ray, Deputy Corcoran, did a little checking and found out that Connor buys about a dozen pairs of glasses at the same time. Tends to lose them I guess."

I sighed. "What does that mean then?"

"I think it means that the glasses aren't the key. It's possible that this style of glasses frames, while you think they're awful, Kathy, are popular. Lots of people might have the same frames or frames that look similar."

I decided right then that the glasses in my blanket chest were meaningless. They're probably the same ones I handed to Miss Janine the day of her fight with Connor and Connor didn't miss them at all because he had so many pairs.

"It means," said Martha breaking into my thoughts, "that whoever has the tenderizer is the killer."

CHAPTER NINETEEN

M Y MOM AND DAD MADE ME go out with them on Saturday night for family night. Martha was right. This was gross.

We went to Janine's Restaurant partly because they loved her food but also because they had a kids menu that my mother liked. Ever since moving to paradise my Mom was into "eating smart, eating right".

I was in the restroom when I heard familiar voices.

"John, I'm tired of this." I dried my hands and leaned my ear against the wall to hear more through the thin walls.

"Otto, we need to discuss this."

I bent down to peer through a knothole in the paneling that Miss Janine had once mentioned needing to fix. I was grateful she hadn't gotten around to it.

"Janine is gone. Dead. Face it." That voice came from Mr. Otto and the other was John Tucker.

"You should have taken better care of her, Otto." John Tucker stood right in front of the hole. Great! Now I couldn't see a thing. I went back to pressing my ear against the wall. Where was a glass when you needed one?

"You listen to me you disgusting pile of nothing," Otto said. "I took great care of Janine. She meant the world to me."

"If you had taken such good care of her she wouldn't be dead now would she?"

I couldn't stand it any more. I had to hear better and watch their facial expressions. I opened the door as quietly as I could and poked my nose around the doorjamb much as I had done the day of Connor's fight with Miss Janine.

Shorter by a head, Mr. Otto had to crane his neck to look into John's eyes. They hadn't noticed me. So far.

"You're drunk, John. Go home. Sleep it off."

"I'm not drunk. I've had just enough to gather the courage to face you, Otto."

"About what John?"

"About LeAnn. And Janine."

I thought I saw the blood drain out of Mr. Otto's face but it could have been bad lighting in the hallway. Mr. Otto looked away from John and down at the floor.

"You think I don't know it was you my wife ran off with?" John whispered. "I know it was you. And then you fooled around with another young girl and got her killed!"

"What?" Otto shrieked. "Who?"

"What? Who?" John said in poor imitation. "You and Janine had a thing going. I seen you two together. You were about to ruin another young life."

Tears ran out of Mr. Otto's eyes and I looked away. I felt embarrassed to be watching something so private but I just had to hear the rest.

"You idiot," Otto said as he removed a handkerchief from his pocket to swipe at his eyes and nose. "You always were a moron, John. Yes, I did go away with LeAnn because she begged me to. I'm not proud of it. Having an affair was wrong but I was young and stupid." Otto let time pass before speaking again. "She was pregnant, John. With Janine."

John Tucker's jaw dropped halfway to the floor, I swear. So did mine.

"Janine was my daughter," Otto said softly, sadly.

"And then I came out of the bathroom," I said to Martha on the phone that night.

"How come you were at Janine's Restaurant?"

"Family date night."

"Oh yuck. So Mr. Otto and Miss Janine were father and daughter? Whoa. Hey, I guess I was right on that one."

"You were. This is going to sound weird," I said. "But, do you think John Tucker killed Janine?"

"No. Why would he do that? He didn't even know her."

"What if it was an accident? Mr. Otto and Miss Janine were about the same height, right?"

"Yeah, I guess," Martha said.

"About the same build," I replied trying to line them up side-by-side in my head. "Haven't you ever guessed wrong about someone's identity from behind? Could John have been so mad at seeing Mr. Otto with a young woman that he felt he needed to take the matter into his own hands? Maybe it reminded him of what happened with his wife."

"But if that were true why stay around here? Wouldn't he leave?"

"Not necessarily. You told me that Mr. Tucker has worked at Warner School for a while. If he left suddenly it could raise some eyebrows. Especially if he left right after Miss Janine's death."

"Yeah," she said. "But would Mr. Tucker have it in him to try to kill Mr. Otto?"

"Maybe if he'd had enough to drink."

CHAPTER TWENTY

A FTER SCHOOL THE FOLLOWING MONDAY, Martha dragged me to John Tucker's office in the hopes of finding something that would tie him to our mystery. We found his office in a far corner of the school and that didn't make me happy. His door was closed.

"Marth, I think we should listen to Miss Fiddler and Deputy Ray. They weren't happy about our going to Oceanside alone and they wouldn't be dancing in the streets now. And Tucker scares me."

"Oh, you big baby. What's he going to do? Kill us?"

"Maybe! Martha, this guy really scares me. He's big and strong. Aren't you the least little bit worried? We're breaking into an office and looking through someone else's things. How would you feel if that happened to you?"

"One," Martha said, holding up a finger, "we're not breaking in we're walking in. See?" She said this as she turned the knob and opened the door to a dark space. "Second, I'm not going through someone else's things." Martha produced a small flashlight from her pocket.

"Not yet," I responded.

We gazed around the small office.

"What are we looking for anyway?" I asked.

"Anything to incriminate John Tucker."

"Really? Incriminate is an awful big word for such little squirts," John Tucker said as he came into the office behind us. "Incriminate me for what, Martha Cunningham?"

The sound of John Tucker's bass voice shocked me. I know I jumped what seemed like a foot in the air and wondered if Martha had too.

"Did I say incriminate?" Martha asked. "I meant nominate. Yeah. Nominate you for an award."

"No you didn't, Martha Cunningham." John Tucker shut and locked the door and drew nearer to us. "What are you two up to in here?"

First, I didn't like the fact that he knew Martha's name. Then I really didn't like that he had closed and locked the door. We were in really huge trouble now. I had to think fast. As fast as I could. And then it came to me.

"We came looking for you sir," I said, hoping that tacking on the 'sir' would help our cause. It didn't.

"For what, I say."

"Computer advice. I understand you're the one to ask. I just got a new computer and I need some programming help."

"I see," he said. Maybe this had bought us some time. For now. He stepped behind his desk, sat down, and opened a drawer. I sucked in my breath at the same time Martha did. John Tucker pulled out a book and said, "Say. Aren't you the girl I saw at Janine's Restaurant last Saturday night?"

"Uh, I'm not sure. Maybe."

"No maybe. I recognize you. You're the girl whose family bought that big fancy house at the end of Cemetery Road. You think you're better than us island folks 'cause your family got money?"

"No. No I don't." I looked over at Martha to get her reaction.

"Don't be looking to her to help you answer a simple question, girl."

No doubt about it. This guy's nuts.

John Tucker rose from his chair and came to stand over me. He was the Empire State Building next to me. Really.

"What did you hear in that bathroom at the restaurant? I remember you coming out the door right about the time we were finishing our discussion."

"I don't know what you're talking about," I lied. Again. It was getting harder to hear anything over the pounding of my own heart.

"Yes you do. How much did you hear?"

A knock at the door caused everyone to jump. "John?" John Tucker didn't respond. He placed a knobby finger up to his mouth ordering us to be quiet.

"He's right here!" Martha called out. John Tucker lunged at her to shut her up.

"Why is this door locked? What's going on?" said the female voice on the other side of the door. "That was a girl's voice I heard John Tucker. Who is in there with you?" The voice sounded like Miss Phelps, the school librarian.

"I'm not done with you two, yet," John Tucker whispered as he opened the door. Miss Phelps stood at the threshold.

"Jill, uh, Miss Phelps. I was talking with Martha and…"

"Kathy," I said, relieved that he couldn't bring my name right into his head.

"Kathy, about computers. Kathy here just got a new machine. Pentium IV, right?"

I've got to give Tucker this: he was quick. He picked up on the computer story and even upped it a bit.

"Uh," I stammered, looking from him to Miss Phelps and back again. "Yes. Right."

Miss Phelps had given us the break that we had needed. Martha and I had managed to get to the door of Tucker's office. The memory of Miss Janine ran through my head. "Mr. Tucker, thanks for your help. May I borrow those manuals some time?"

He smiled too sweetly. He was clearly embarrassed in front of Miss Phelps and was all too quick to let us leave. "Kathy, any time. Just stop me in the hall when you're ready and I'll drop them off with your teacher."

"Miss Fiddler," I said.

"Right. Miss Fiddler. Room 6. Thanks, girls."

Martha and I left his office as quickly as we could without drawing attention to ourselves and the last thing we heard was the snap of his door closing. I turned around to see that Miss Phelps had disappeared inside the lion's den.

CHAPTER TWENTY-ONE

ANOTHER FRIDAY NIGHT but this one's different. After the run-in with Mr. Tucker, my imagination was starting to run wild. I didn't know who to talk to about it. Mom and Dad were busy. They're always "busy" these days. I got more of their time when Dad worked full-time and Mom part-time when we lived in New Jersey.

I had tried to talk to them about this but Mom said it's just me. She said she's available any time but whenever something came up, I couldn't seem to find her even if she was in the same room. You know?

I wish Miss Janine were still here. I could talk with her.

"Everyone has secrets, Kath," Miss Janine said. "Whether there's something physical to hide," she said, smiling at me, "or emotional, we all have them and we all feel that we wouldn't be accepted should they get out."

We sat at the small round table just inside the back door to the kitchen. Miss Janine had made fruit smoothies in the blender. Mine was just the way I liked it: lots of crushed ice, strawberries, banana, orange juice and vanilla yogurt. I wasn't so sure about the yogurt part until Miss Janine had goaded me into trying one.

It was 3:00 in the afternoon, the only time the restaurant

ever seemed quiet. "I hate it when people look at me with pity. Like I wanted my hand to be this way so I didn't have to do as much as other kids."

"Are some kids afraid of you?"

"I think so. Some kids won't even talk to me. That happened a lot in New Jersey and it's happening here, too."

"Fear's a funny thing. We all go around wanting people to like us and are afraid that if someone finds out some secret you have, well, it'll just blow the whole thing."

"What about **your** hand?"

Miss Janine stared into her smoothie and I thought I saw tears dot the corners of her eyes.

"Miss Janine?"

"Did I ever tell you that I almost didn't open this restaurant because of my hand?"

"No."

"Well, it's true. It was Mr. Otto who convinced me that it didn't matter whether or not I had full use of my hand. It mattered that the food tasted good and people enjoyed themselves."

"I think people like to come here."

"I do too. Now."

I waited for her to speak again.

"I was afraid, Kathy. I don't have an obvious deformity like you do but there are some things I can't do very well and I was worried that any staff I had hired would think I was a slacker..."

"Slacker?"

"Not pulling my own weight. Making others do things for me for whatever reason." She reached over and pulled my left hand up. "You gotta let them look, Kath."

I looked down at my misshapen hand, the one I had hidden from myself all of my life. "This is part of who you are. Doesn't make you a bad person, just different. You project the fear and distrust because you don't trust yourself to deal with the situation." She looked into my eyes. "Maybe this is too advanced for you."

"No," I said softly, still staring at my hand.

"The only way to get rid of the stares is to give people their fear. Let them be grossed out, let them feel bad for you. And then let them move on. If they want to know Kathy, like I do, they'll come around. You have to let people be afraid. Let people feel what they feel."

Remembering that day helped me want to solve this mystery more than ever. Let people feel what they feel. It sounded like good sense to me then and it sounded like good sense to me now. I could always count on her to talk straight with me.

Right now Mr. Tucker scares me and I don't know what to think about Connor and Mr. Otto. But somebody killed my friend and I want to be the one to solve it.

Solving this mystery reminded me of another: Martha's house.

"I'm tired of going to my house. Let's go to your house this afternoon," I said to Martha as we walked home from school. Every time I suggested we go to her house I got the same answer: it's a mess.

Martha sighed dramatically and rolled her eyes upward. "No can do. Carmella's taking a cooking class and the house is a mess."

I shrugged. "I don't care." Something didn't add up to me and I pressed Martha harder. "Wait a minute. I thought money was so tight you could barely breathe. How can she take a cooking class?"

"Did I say cooking class? I meant she's practicing her cooking. She's not very good, you know" Martha whispered, leaning in to me.

"No, I wouldn't know. I never get to go to your house. For anything! Come on. It doesn't matter what your house looks like. I'd just like to go."

"Why?" Martha had stopped walking and stood, facing me, with one bunched up fist on her hip. "What's the big rush to see my house?"

"No rush. I just think it would be nice to share that part of your life. No big deal. Let's go to my house."

We strolled the rest of the way to my house that afternoon, with Martha gabbing on about the latest TV show she'd seen.

But tomorrow, I was bound and determined to find out why Martha Cunningham never let me visit her house.

CHAPTER TWENTY-TWO

SATURDAY MORNING DAWNED bright and clear, one of those Warner days that the locals said they waited for. Not a cloud in the sky, warm but not hot, no humidity, soft ocean breeze. Today, Mom was right: this was paradise.

I walked over to Martha's. Along the way I looked at the flower boxes and gardens of the summer cottages. Most of them would close for the winter soon. I decided to ask Mr. Otto if I could help with the kitchen garden at Miss Janine's next year. He had once told me that she was the only one who liked to take care of it. I'd like to remember Miss Janine by caring for her garden.

Martha sat on the front stoop of her trailer with her mother. They were snapping green beans and laughing. Mrs. Cunningham removed the tips of the beans with her thumbnail and then gave them to Martha to break in half and throw into the bowl at her feet. I can't remember the last time I sat with my mom like that.

"Hi," I said, as I strolled up to them.

I had expected Martha's reaction: shock mixed with worry.

"Hey, Kathy," said Mrs. Cunningham loudly. "So nice to finally see you over here. I've been telling Martha to have you over but she said you were always too busy."

I shot Martha a look but she missed it.

"Well, so good to see you. I've got to get ready for work." Mrs. Cunningham took the unfinished snap beans with her and left us alone.

"Your mom has to work a lot, huh?" I asked.

"Yeah. My brother's braces are expensive."

"You told me that. How about your dad? Does he help out?"

"Don't know where he is."

"Oh. Sorry."

"How did you find me?"

"It's not rocket science. I followed you home one day. It's no bog deal, as Carmella would say. Can we talk?" Martha got up from the stoop and opened the door for me to enter. I stood in a pretty living room decorated in shades of tan, blue and gray.

"Why didn't you tell me that you knew I lived in trailer trash haven?"

"Because you had to want to tell me yourself. And I don't think its trailer trash haven. There are some neat artists who live here. After the first few times you gave me excuses for not playing at your house I got curious. You don't have to be embarrassed in front of me. I'm your friend."

"I know it isn't what you're used to. I want to live in a big fancy house like yours someday. You have tons of money and I don't."

"My parents have money not me. And we didn't always live like we do now. Our house in New Jersey was small and dark." Martha hadn't let us move from in front of the front door.

"You didn't?"

"No. My Dad sold his liquor store because somebody named his price."

"But you have it all! Beautiful room, new computer, cool bike." Martha's head hung down.

"Booby prizes."

"Huh?"

"Booby prizes. You know. Don't make a fuss over this move, Kathy, and we'll give you whatever you want. Back home, I begged my parents for a room makeover for a whole year. You think we have money? You should see how some of my friends in New Jersey live!"

"Don't you get everything you ask for?"

"No way! I get five bucks a week allowance. I want something, I have to earn it."

"I thought you had the good life and if you knew where I lived you would stop being my friend."

"And I thought you wouldn't be my friend once you saw where I lived. That my parent's money made me snobby or something."

"Well, I guess we were both wrong. Come on. I'll show you my room."

I followed Martha down a hallway as she pointed out the rooms along the way. The trailer was long and wide. The door to Martha's room bore a hand-painted warning sign: "Enter at your own risk."

Her room was a shrine to the sixties complete with black light and multi-colored bead curtain. I wandered around the room taking in all of the interesting things she had. One entire wall had shelves full of paperback books.

"Tell me again why you like the sixties so much," I said, perching on a nearby stool.

Martha sat on a bed covered with a colorful cotton bedspread. She shrugged and bit her thumbnail. "My mom was happy in the sixties. She said that she had her whole life ahead of her, women were starting to do more things instead of staying home raising kids, and she wanted to go to art school. She had dreams."

"What happened after the sixties?"

"She met my dad. My grandparents hated him so she ran

off with him. Didn't go to art school. Not long after I was born, my dad took off. She said that he went out for some milk and a loaf of bread and never came back. She still doesn't know what happened to him, she just knows that he left her with two young kids. And what my grandparents had warned her about had come true."

Martha and I were quiet for a moment.

"I want her to be happy again," Martha said.

I didn't know what to say. I played with the beads on the curtain next to me. "I love this curtain! I think I'll save for one." I drew the strands out and then let them fall back into place. "I'm scared of Mr. Tucker, Marth. And I don't know what to think of Mr. Otto and Connor."

"Me, too."

"I do know this. We need to solve this mystery. For Miss Janine."

"Well, what do we know? We know that Mr. Otto says he's Janine's father, that Mr. Tucker was married to the woman Mr. Otto ran off with, and that Connor has hurt Miss Janine in the past."

"Who can we rule out?"

"I don't think Connor had anything to do with it, honestly."

"But I saw him grab her!"

"Yes, but would he kill her over a recipe? What would killing her do?"

I couldn't answer that question.

"Mr. Tucker, on the other hand..."

"Mr. Tucker has been number one in my book since yesterday," I said. "I never seriously considered Mr. Otto anyway. I've seen him with her. If he is her father, his affection for her makes sense."

Martha's face showed her concentration. "We need to find the tenderizer. We need to go to Mr. Tucker's house."

CHAPTER TWENTY-THREE

S O NOW WE'RE BACK to where we started. I'm on my belly on the floor of John Tucker's yucky trailer looking at Martha's little toes peeking out of the sides of her sneakers. And by now you probably know that the art object I first saw when we walked into this palace of garbage was the tenderizer I used to use at Janine's.

Also known as the murder weapon. Or at least what we all thought of as the murder weapon.

"I knew you weren't looking for computer advice when I caught you two in my office. Now I've got the both of you for breaking and entering."

"Not breaking," Martha said.

"Huh?"

"Not breaking. Just entering. You left your door unlocked." Martha skipped only a beat before she continued. "Why did you do it?"

"Do what?"

"You know."

By this time I had risen to my knees when John Tucker saw my eye lock on the tenderizer.

"What are you so interested in? This?" he asked as he

picked it up and shook it in my face like a baby's rattle. I couldn't keep my eyes from it.

I watched as Tucker bounced it in his beefy hand and then slammed it down. "What do you know?" he shouted at me.

He pulled me to my feet by my left elbow and you know what that did to my hand.

"What?" he shrieked. He looked down at my hand and then shoved it in my face. "You're a cripple? **That's** why you always have it stuck in your pocket? Little cripple trying to act the big detective. What a joke."

That did it. This slime ball was not going to make fun of my disability or me. I cracked. "I'm not a cripple!" I screamed. I got right in his face. I'm not sure what made me do it; I could have really been hurt. "I have a disability. What I choose to do with it or about it is my business."

My outburst set him back for just a second. I knew this because he didn't say anything right away.

"Don't smart-mouth me, cripple," he said as he hefted the tenderizer once again. He pushed me against the nearest wall.

"Leave her alone," Martha pleaded, trying to pull him away from me.

"Are you going to bash my head in just like you did Miss Janine's? Or did you really think you were killing Mr. Otto?" I asked, faster than I had time to think. His eyes opened wider and I knew then that I had gotten it just right.

John Tucker elbowed Martha propelling her toward the kitchen. Out of the corner of my eye I saw her pick up a dirty cast iron fry pan and, using both hands, slammed it into his right knee.

He lost his grip on the tenderizer and me. Martha managed to swing back and get him again as his eyes filled with rage.

"That's enough, Martha," Deputy Ray Corcoran said.

"That's enough."

After John Tucker had been led away in handcuffs and tears, Deputy Ray offered us a ride home.

"Thanks, Deputy Corcoran, but I think I'd like to walk," I said.

"You can call me Ray, Kathy, that's okay. Martha, what about you? You want to walk, too?""

"Yes. But, Ray?"

"Yeah," said Ray as he watched a Sheriff's car drive off with John Tucker in the back seat.

"What really happened to John Tucker?"

"He said that he never meant to kill anyone, he had been drinking. He always thought Janine was his child and then was furious when Otto claimed paternity. Tucker never believed that by the way. He thought that Otto was trying to fool around with Janine just like he did with LeAnn, Tucker's ex-wife. When he got to the restaurant that night, he saw someone he thought was Otto, picked up the tenderizer and starting hitting this individual over the head with it. It wasn't until he read the next day's paper that he realized what he had done and to whom."

"I read an article that said Mr. Tucker was a computer genius," I said. "Why was he the school janitor?" I asked.

"He was shattered without his wife. Probably thought no one would ever be interested in him because he was divorced. And without a wife he wouldn't have children. He said he loved kids."

"Not the way he treated us he didn't," Martha interjected.

"John Tucker was afraid," said Deputy Ray. "Let's just leave it at that, okay?"

"I'm glad you got here when you did, Deputy Ray. How'd you know?" I asked.

"Your pal here left me a note at the station. Just lucky I saw it when I did."

Martha and I nodded in agreement and watched as Ray slid into the driver's seat of his squad car. His tires kicked up a rooster tail of dust as he drove down the road away from us.

CHAPTER TWENTY-FOUR

SO JOHN TUCKER CONFESSED to murder," I said coming to the end of my story. Everyone one at the picnic table was staring at me.

"Did anyone figure out who Janine's father really was?" Jeb Seely asked.

"The paper said that according to blood tests taken from the crime scene and samples taken from John Tucker, it wasn't clear."

"You mean John Tucker might have killed his own daughter?" asked a blonde girl named Heather.

"Maybe," Martha said.

"Kathy, can we see your hand?" Jeb asked.

I took a deep breath and removed my hand from my shorts pocket. My four classmates looked at it in earnest.

And I let them do it.

I watched Jeb's face as he studied my fingers and then my thumb. He nodded to himself as though he were finally satisfied. Noise from a game of kickball broke the silence.

"Okay you two," said Jeb to Martha and me. "Let's get a team together. I want Harmon and Cunningham," he called to the other team leader.

After picking his team, Jeb held our attention in a semi-huddle. "Martha, you and Tom stay to Kathy's left. Leave anything on the right to her. That's her strong side," he said, grinning at me.

I looked at Martha. Just before we started to play she pulled me aside, smiled and said, "I've got something for you." She reached into her pocket and pulled out the MIA bracelet.

"That's your favorite thing in the whole world! I can't take this. It was your uncle's."

"You're the best friend I've ever had, Kat."

"Come on, Marth. You've got lots of friends."

"Lots of acquaintances, maybe. But you're really my best friend. Nobody else would get into trouble with me. I feel like I've known you all of my life."

"Thanks," I said, smiling broadly. "You're my best friend, too."

Martha held out the bracelet. I hesitated only a moment before slipping it on my left wrist.

THE END